Swamp

Sloan grabb̶e̶d̶ ̶t̶h̶e̶ ̶l̶a̶u̶n̶c̶h̶er and sighted a grenade with a combination armor-piercing and fragmentation head on the lead FSE hovercraft.

As he judged its forward speed the lead craft opened fire. Its turret weapon was a twenty-millimeter Gatling gun. It made a noise like the *wow* of a disc jockey cueing a record magnified a million times.

A section of the swamp just disintegrated. A whirlwind of high explosives stripped away a hundred square meters of vegetation in the blink of an eye. By ill luck the first burst had found the hiding place of part of Sloan's team. Sam saw a man crouching in knee-deep water suddenly come apart like a glass jar dropped on a brick floor, shattered by the impact. The terrible force of the weapon picked up an airboat and flipped it and the occupant backwards, both being shredded by the bullet storm into splintered planks and flaming fuel and streamers of bloody flesh.

THE GUARDIANS
AMERICA'S FUTURE IS IN THEIR HANDS

*Also in THE GUARDIANS series
from Jove*

THE GUARDIANS
TRIAL BY FIRE
THUNDER OF HELL
NIGHT OF THE PHOENIX
ARMAGEDDON RUN
WAR ZONE

THE GUARDIANS
BRUTE FORCE

RICHARD AUSTIN

A JOVE BOOK

THE GUARDIANS: BRUTE FORCE

A Jove Book / published by arrangement with
the author

PRINTING HISTORY
Jove edition / January 1987

ISBN: 0–515–08836–6

For Chip

CHAPTER
ONE ————————————————

With a shriek like the sky bursting open, artillery rounds arced in to tear vast chunks out of the rolling Indiana countryside on either side of the convoy. "Christ on a crutch," said Billy McKay, as much in disgust as anything else, while the driver beside him spun the wheel frantically, trying to straighten out the Winnebago on the narrow country road from which shell bursts had nearly knocked it.

"Billy? Are you, like, all right?" Casey Wilson, mellow as always, said in his ear. The lanky ex–fighter jock was stacked behind the wheel of Mobile One, hanging back to delay pursuit from the company-sized Effsee unit whose fringes they had brushed fifty or sixty klicks northeast of Evansville.

"That's affirmative," McKay replied, his words picked up by the little fleshtone microphone taped to his larynx. "No big deal. Just three tubes, and they ain't shooting too

1

good." He didn't mention that with two 105s and a 155-millimeter firing, they wouldn't *have* to shoot too good. No point in worrying the boy.

They were lucky, however, that the enemy was just a ragtag remnant of the Federated States of Europe's expeditionary force, which was in the process of collapsing like a busted bubblegum bubble on its headquarters in California; just pure chickenshit luck to have brushed up against this group. Armed with ordnance that was probably liberated from National Guard armories, they would not be employing any fancy time-on-target or sheaving techniques here. The expeditionary force had always been a pretty shoestring operation. Nor had the force that Chairman Maximov had sent across the Atlantic in late winter ever been exactly elite, consisting largely of scapegrace units Maximov preferred to have absent from a European empire wracked by civil disturbances—a few thousand mouths the FSE wouldn't have to feed in times of crushing shortage.

On the other hand, the Guardians' convoy consisted of a couple of big, lumbering soft-skin vehicles and some makeshift combat cars out of DC's Tide Camp. It wouldn't take a lot of luck or skill on the part of Effsee gunners to put the Guardians and their charges to some serious hurt.

"Sloan?" McKay asked. "Any problems?"

From the big orange school bus bouncing along behind the Winnebago, former Navy Commander Sam Sloan jauntily replied, "Negative, McKay. It's just another example of your basic landlubber accuracy; we couldn't be safer in a battleship." As a man who had had his baptism of fire as the gunnery-control officer on the cruiser *Winston-Salem*, Sloan pretended disdain for both the gunnery skills and firepower of ground forces.

"Want us to look and see if we can hunt down those tubes?" another voice asked hungrily. Tyler, leader of the squad of Tide Camp warriors sent along to help escort the

Blueprint for Renewal personnel from Luxor, Iowa, to the relative safety of the nation's capital, was spoiling for a fight. As usual.

"Negative. You stick close. But you can send an out-rider or two to see if you can scope out who's spotting those rounds." That was bothering McKay, who the Eff-sees' forward observer was. Lacking in pinpoint accuracy though they were, the FSE tubes weren't just shooting at engine noise. Until their FO was taken out, they'd keep shooting—and Effsees had to get lucky sometime.

The carnival atmosphere aboard Sloan's bus evaporated abruptly with the first trio of shells. "Everybody down!" Sloan shouted even as the incoming mail was still whistling down on them, furiously regretting that they hadn't at least taped the windows to mitigate the danger of flying glass splinters.

Obediently, everybody ducked, except of course the Tide Camp driver and Sloan himself, who'd been standing facing back down the bus with his butt perched on the rail that ran behind the driver's seat, playing scoutmaster to what was probably the highest-powered assemblage of engineers, scientists, and sundry other expert-types in the nation's history. At the last instant he had thrown up his arm to shield his eyes, trusting to the Kevlar vest inside his steel-gray fatigue coveralls to save him from serious harm if the shell bursts punched the windows in. Miraculously, the windows stayed intact.

Now he stood, rocking slightly, his heart fluttering at the base of his throat as if he'd tried to swallow a pigeon, giving the lie to the wiseass nonchalance of his exchange with McKay. Heads began tentatively to poke up from behind cracked dirt-brown seatbacks, men and women, few of them any too young, to disentangle themselves from a heap on the corrugated, mud-tracked runner in the aisle.

From somewhere in the back of the bus an Aiwa boombox some joker had tuned to KFSU in Oklahoma City blared nasal hayseed gospel into echoing emptiness.

I should have known it couldn't be this easy, Sloan thought.

After their last confrontation with the Witch-King of the Ruins—better known to the *cognoscenti* as Colonel Ivan Vesensky, late of the KGB—the situation in the nation's once and future capital had stabilized with almost frightening speed. Raggedy-assed and desperate-eyed as most of the survivor groups crawling through the DC rubble were, a lot of them perceived they had a lot more to gain from life's settling down than from throwing in with the holdouts in a cause that amounted to little more than raising hell for hell's own sake. The real backbone of opposition to the alliance the Guardians were trying to weld together, Malcom Jabbar's New Nation of Islam, Inc., had been shattered in the confrontations at the Villa Firenza and the Capitol. The remainder, dead-end gangs who'd fallen under the Witch-King's sway, got mopped up, surrendered, or slunk away to lick their wounds.

The end of a serious external threat wasn't the end of problems in the capital, by any means. Some members of the still-shaky alliance had been mortal enemies mere weeks before, and some of them—Seth Rushton's American Union people came to mind—had actually been pretty closely allied to Jabbar. And the Guardians' chief ally, the forces in charge at this very moment of securing President Jeffery MacGregor in the White House, were the Tide Camp warriors of the enigmatic Soong; and they, as McKay said, were a pretty funny bunch. But they were devoted to Soong, who was devoted to the President, and for the rest, that was all politics and diplomacy and thank God out of the Guardians' hands.

By late August the Guardians had been ready for the next big step: moving the personnel of the top-secret Blueprint, whom they'd assembled so painstakingly in the seven months after the One-Day War—the ones who had survived the destruction of Heartland Complex, at any rate —to their new headquarters in Washington. The business of rebuilding America, so rudely interrupted by the FSE invasion and the bizarre but brief return of Wild Bill Lowell as President of the United States and puppet to Chairman Maximov, needed urgently to be resumed. While tools and factories and canned food overall survived the bombing and its aftermath much better than the human population, the cushion of surplus was growing thinner every day; stockpiles and scavenging would eventually play out. And the major functional Blueprint facility actually recovered, the New Eden lab-commune in California, which was intended to supply tons of genetically altered miracle seeds to a shattered nation, had fallen into the hands of the FSE.

The situation wasn't desperate. Not yet. The American people had proven far more resilient than anyone gave them credit for, at least the survivors. But if America was not to enter a new Dark Age, or fall under the sway of Maximov's legions, the Blueprint braintrust had to start firing on all cylinders, and soon. That meant the Guardians had to resume their task of searching out more Blueprint personnel immediately—just as soon as the ones they'd found already were safely in Washington.

Luxor was no sweat. The remaining FSE garrisons that dotted the country were getting very introspective now, readying for their own pullback to the West Coast, the units ordered to remain growing daily more conscious that the odds were lengthening against them. The Federated States' expedition had always been as much a plundering raid as an actual attempt to conquer and hold, even when they had Wild Bill as a figurehead. They'd done none too good a job of winning American hearts and minds. Hell, according to the word from the Guardians' hacker buddies in Colorado's Freehold and in occupied California, plus what information they were able to glean themselves with the White House communications gear and the Expeditionary Force codes they'd captured with their new Mobile One, Maximov's boys weren't doing too hot a job of that in Europe.

But trouble of a sort had awaited the Guardians in Luxor, although the Luxorians had been happy as always to see them. For their part, the people of Luxor had shared unstintingly with the outsiders, even in these none-too-flush times. These Iowa farmers had suffered less than most, however, and what they had, they shared. To their natural generosity was added the tremendous debt they bore the Guardians, and their belief, quiet and strong, in the necessity of rebuilding America.

But when the time came to move out, the Blueprint personnel simply went on strike. They were not military personnel or hardy retreaters. They were specialists, office dwellers for the most part, accustomed almost to a man and woman to soft lives before the war.

Since the war, life had been hard for everybody, but those chosen to take part in Project Blueprint had found it even harder than most. They had undergone the same hardships as the populace at large before the Guardians collected them and conveyed them back to Heartland. Some hadn't made it. Others, like Dr. Mark Bollear, rescued by the Guardians from cannibals in the badlands of South Dakota, had experienced some pretty close scrapes. For a time after recovery, they enjoyed the secure and plentiful—if restricted—life of the vast underground complex called Heartland. Then came the FSE takeover and a Babylonian captivity that involved fear and hardship for all and, for some, torture.

Capping it all off had been a midnight rescue from Heartland by the Guardians and their motley allies, a wild run through hills and woods with the complex erupting like a volcano at their backs as it self-destructed, culminating in a brief, savage meeting engagement with a column of Effsee troups. They had, to put it bluntly, had enough.

"It's not that we wish to be uncooperative," said former Harvard economist Dr. Marguerite Connoly, the inevitable spokesperson for the group, who was not notorious for acting any other way when getting any other way than her own. "But we simply cannot ride all the way to Washington jouncing about in the bed of a truck."

Ex-Marine Billy McKay, the Guardians' leader, linebacker sized and as short-fused as a concussion grenade, had predictably gone off in her face, turning bright red, waving his piledriver fists, and bellowing like the Parris Island drill instructor he used to be. It was the wrong move. Connoly just faced him down with her arms folded across the front of her red checked Pendleton shirt and her pug nose aloofly elevated, until he played himself out and had no choice but to stomp off into the darkness and chew sullenly on his stub of cigar.

Sam Sloan and Casey Wilson had learned not even to try to talk to their leader when he was in this mood. It was left for the fourth Guardian, soft-spoken Tom Rogers, a shadow-warface ace with fifteen years of dirty missions for the Green Berets under his belt, to reason with him. Though the months of rigorous Guardians training and the payoff year of shared and almost uninterrupted danger since the war had forged close bonds of trust and confidence among all the Guardians, Rogers was still the teammate whose judgment McKay respected the most.

He was also the team medical officer, which gave him a certain leverage even over his chief. "These folks ain't young, Billy," he said in his soft Southern drawl, picked up during the peripatetic life of an Army brat. "Most of them are fifty, or pushing it. And we got to get them to Washington in good working order."

McKay muttered something about candy-assed civilians. "Shit. It ain't even a thousand miles."

"Come on, Billy." Rogers spoke with the mildest of emphasis, which was equivalent to most men grabbing somebody by the front of the shirt and giving them a good shake. Unlike most men, Rogers had all the balls he needed to do just that to Billy McKay, who had six inches and almost eighty pounds on him; and unlike most men he had not a bad chance of living to tell about it. But that wasn't his style. "You busted your butt in plenty of trucks. None of these folks would have any kidneys worth mentioning inside of three hundred klicks, and their lower backs would be knocked all to heck, and their joints—"

But McKay was already waving his hands and shaking his head in surrender. So they spent an extra week, as the days got shorter and the sunlight more golden, salvaging and refitting a couple of more appropriate vehicles.

They had finally cruised out of Luxor two days ago, taking it easy. Most of the scientists were in the alcohol-burning bus, with what little baggage they had strapped along with foodstuffs and medical supplies on the roof, and a couple of big spare tanks of alky bolted on the back—given alcohol's much lesser explosive power, a much smaller risk than carrying spare gasoline would have been. A privileged few, however—Dr. Marguerite Connoly and her four closest confidants—got to ride in the much plusher confines of a big recreational vehicle, similarly equipped with auxiliary alcohol tanks. They had, inevitably, been dubbed the "kitchen cabinet," and they were the ones the mayor of Luxor had been the happiest to see the last of—the ones who expected to set up shop on arrival in Washington as Jeff MacGregor's closest advisors.

• • •

By this afternoon the lesser mortals riding in what they termed the back of the bus had mostly quit griping about the fact and were singing kids' summer camp songs, of all things, when the school bus radio crackled into stammering life. One of Tyler's outriders, mounted on a scrambler bike, had spotted uniformed men moving quickly away through a clump of trees off to their left. A few seconds later they all heard the distant popping of gunfire over the weary chug of the bus's engine.

A moment later Casey was on the horn from Mobile One. The computerized channel-scan had picked up a considerable amount of abrupt, startled traffic on Expeditionary Force freeks, and the onboard computer had sampled signal strengths and announced that the bad guys were quite close by.

At McKay's command, the two lumbering passenger vehicles put the pedal to the metal and took off down the road as fast as they could, while Casey slewed Mobile One off onto the red-clay shoulder and went zooming back toward the rise they'd just crested. By this stage of the game almost all Effsee transport was soft-skinned; any kind of tracked vehicle is a bitch to maintain in the field, and spare drive-train parts or even replacement treads weren't exactly easy to come by in the world after the Holocaust. The ten-ton armored car, with its .50-caliber machine gun and fully automatic forty-millimeter grenade launcher in its turret, carried enough firepower to discourage serious pursuit by anything short of tanks.

Sloan waved to Casey as the V-450 chugged past. The former fighter ace waved back through an open top hatch before slamming it down. Sloan repressed a shudder. He remembered the first—and last—time the Guardians had come up against an Effsee tank. It was why they'd needed a new Mobile One. They'd almost needed a new Casey Wilson.

A couple more of Tyler's tough but wild vets bounced after the big car on dirt bikes, to serve as auxiliary eyes and ears. Sloan was just thinking they'd got clean away when the incoming mail arrived.

"We've got to get off the road," the driver shouted. He was a slight, dark, sharp-faced young man in green cammies with a rag knotted around his temples and a Chiricahua war-stripe painted across his nose.

Apparently Sloan's throat mike picked up the words, because a half second later McKay's voice bellowed, "Belay that!" over the bus CB and the bone-conduction phone taped behind his left ear, rattling the radio speaker and damn near taking Sam's head off at the jawline.

The driver grabbed his own mike. "They've got the road targeted! We got to get off it!"

"Bullshit. Why would they do that? They got spotters on us. We go slogging off cross-country, they're going to pick us off. Speed's what we need."

From behind came the sound of Mobile One's big MG. To old Missouri farmboy Sam Sloan, the ponderous, authoritative pounding of the guns sounded like nothing so much as somebody driving steel spikes with a sledgehammer a few hundred yards away. "Contact, Billy," said Rogers's voice. "Tried to push Silverado up out of a gully. We nailed 'em."

Sloan glanced back in time to see a gob of smoke like a cotton ball painted black roll upward into the sky from behind a hill. He felt a giddy surge of triumph. Even he, surface sailor from way back that he was, knew that piling a bunch of squaddies into the back of a pickup truck wasn't any way to pursue any kind of armed enemy. It argued comforting incompetence on the part of the pursuers—and a frantic haste that indicated the Effsees had an altogether too good idea just who their quarry was.

The radio crackled out a report from the scouts who'd faded back with the armored car. The driver whooped and hit his fists on the big wide steering wheel. "Assholes! Those fuckers ain't got a chance!"

The road ahead of them erupted in flame and smoke and shattered asphalt.

The blast blew in the windows at the rear of the big RV **and** filled the thing with blooming overpressure that popped all the other windows right out. An invisible fist of concussion slammed McKay face-first into the padded dash as the vehicle veered crazily off the road. *I've come through all this just to get my ass shot off in a War Winnebago?* he wondered.

The vehicle heeled dangerously left. Thumps and cries came from the spacious rear. Biting his lower lip so hard a trickle of blood ran down his chin, McKay's driver fought the thing back onto the road, got it upright again.

In back a man's voice was moaning, "Oh my God, oh my God, oh my God," over and over in a broken-record litany.

"For heaven's sake, Richard," rapped Dr. Marguerite Connoly, stern as a schoolmistress and not at all fazed by the near-miss. "Get a hold of yourself." The chant stopped.

"Jesus," McKay rasped. "Sam? Are you all right?"

Sam Sloan was still standing there, up to the front of the bus with his back to the driver and feeling very stunned and foolish. Had the shock of the roadway blowing up almost beneath the bus's front tires not locked him where he stood, he would have been thrown head over heels by the squealing swerve the driver executed to avoid the crater.

Tires howling, the bus skidded broadside for thirty meters. He felt like a plaster-cast statue, standing as if immovable, his left arm braced against the metal upright, sleeve shredded by glass blown from the windshield. Miraculously, the driver had not been blinded by the flying fragments. He drove grimly on, his camouflage blouse in slowly reddening tatters, his face looking as if it had been scratched by harpies.

Sloan became aware of a buzzing in his head, realized that aside from that all he heard was silence, awful and absolute. *Are my eardrums gone?* he wondered fearfully. There was no question that for the moment at least he'd been deafened by the explosion. Fortunately, the little speaker fastened to the mastoid process behind his ear set up vibrations in his skullbone itself; he didn't *need* eardrums to hear it. All he needed was for his brains to sort themselves out before he recognized the voice of Billy McKay loudly and profanely demanding to know if he was still in one piece.

"Why—yeah, Billy," he said. Sheepishness was beginning to set in. He was a missile-and-big-gun Navy man, who had had the bridge of the *Winston-Salem* pretty much sheared off right over his head by a Soviet missile fired from a Libyan boat, and here he was petrified like a jack-lighted deer by a love tap from a landlubber howitzer.

The bus was as full of screaming and lamentations as a Ken Russell flick, but Sloan didn't see anyone actually hurt. "That was just a lucky hit. The other two fell short by a good two hundred meters," he reported coolly, pleased to be able to offer at least this much evidence of his professionalism.

He heard McKay checking for casualties with Tyler over the cadre channel of their pocket-calculator–sized communicators. The Tide Camp contingent had five scouts on motorcycles, two of them now back watching Mobile One duel with the advance elements of the FSE unit they'd bumped. The rest of the thirty-odd men were packed into seven so-called combat cars, several of which had M-249 Squad Automatic Weapon machine guns set on jury-rigged mounts, with Tyler's car now in the lead and the others pulling drag behind the little convoy. A couple of troopers had suffered minor cuts from shell fragments, but there were no serious casualties.

Almost at once another barrage crashed in, this one well behind. However the Effsees were spotting them, the guns weren't coordinating too well with their observers. Sloan allowed himself a grin at the amateurishness of it all.

Hearing returned gradually, like water dripping into a rain barrel. The first thing Sam heard was a twangy voice singing something about Jesus from the speakers of the radio. The next was a low burring of sound all around the periphery of his perception, vague but somehow distinct from the droning of the bus's engine and the babbling-brook sound of tires thrown out of alignment by violent maneuvering. He blinked, figuring the noise for a subjective buzz in his own head.

"What's that noise?" one of the scientists asked, her head rising like an undernourished moon from behind the back of a seat.

Several other heads poked up, began to crane around. "The show's not gonna seem half so interesting if you get your heads cut off by shrapnel," Sloan remarked. The heads vanished again.

"I hear it too," the driver said.

Sloan's first thought was that the Effsees had end-run Mobile One and were hot on their trail. Even he knew a one-vehicle roadblock wasn't any too damn hard to bypass. "*Casey, Tom,*" he said, subvocalizing so that his throat mike would catch the words without anyone else hearing —no point in putting ideas into these good people's heads, now, was there? "How hard are they pushing you? None of them have gotten past you, have they?"

"Negative, Sam," Casey said. "Somebody fired a LAW at us, but the range was too long and it went ballistic. We're, kinda like, getting some small-arms fire, but not too much of that."

Ahead the road rolled straight up a gentle swell of ground. "What's the matter, Sloan, got ants in your pants?" McKay asked. Then the Winnebago crested the rise. "Holy shit!"

Then the bus rolled over the top and there they were, not just on the road ahead but curving out to left and right like the open jaws of a giant insect: road gypsies. Lots of them.

CHAPTER
TWO ─────────────────────────

The road gypsies were nomads who, in the disordered dying days of the 1980s, had decided to adopt a lifestyle from a series of after-the-holocaust adventure flicks. The gypsies had shown a surprising durability when it came time to translate their highway-marauder role playing into reality after the Holocaust. They adopted a range of styles of dress and personal ornamentation as varied as Plains Indians. Their vehicles were the same weird mixed bag: motorcycles, powered trikes, cars stripped to bare bones, dune buggies built out of scrap.

By this stage of the game they were pretty well armed. McKay just had time to reflect that if they had prepared any kind of decent ambush they'd have a great chance of cleaning the Guardians' clocks for them. But that wasn't the gypsies' approach; their whole lifestyle was built on driving fast and acting crazy, so that was how they were damn well gonna do it.

"What's going on?" asked one of the male administrators riding with Connoly in the Winnebago. His hair stuck out in weird clumps to the sides, making his head look like a ragged mushroom. "Who are these people?"

"You don't wanna know," McKay said, trying to fumble his lightweight M-60 machine gun out from between his seat and the driver's. Engines roared up around them like water sloshing into a glass washing-machine tank, such as McKay had seen on TV commercials as a kid. Right nearby he heard the voiceless snarl of a Minimi machine gun on one of the Tide Camp cars. The sound always put him in mind of one of those compressed-gas BB machine guns you see in midways. "Get *down*."

He put his hand on the man's shrunken chest and sent him staggering back to fall down among tangled bedding and baggage and his fellow future molders and shapers of the new America. If they got out of this, Maggie Connoly was going to chew on McKay's ass some for laying hands on one of her precious brain-boys, but he'd crush that cockroach when he came to it.

Everything flashed through his mind in a chaotic fraction of a second, like a shower of sparks from a short circuit. The black steel machine gun was hung up on a protrusion or the frame of the seat or something, and he was still trying to cuss and force it free when there was a twitch of motion in the corner of his eye and a hearty thump on the flat flush front of the Winnebago as a road gypsy came off his dune buggy and leaped onto the big boxy vehicle like a monkey hitting the bars of his cage.

McKay had a wild impression of spiked hair and mad staring eyes and rotten breath as the man clambered through the vacant windshield with a chromed butcher knife in his teeth. Twisted around in his seat to untangle his machine gun, McKay lashed his right hand around in a furious backfist that grazed the driver's ear and smashed into the grinning, painted, distorted face. The gypsy disappeared with a shriek, followed instantly by a double thump and lurch as the wheels went over him.

Blood from the gash the knife had made in the back of McKay's hand spattered the fawn-colored dashboard padding. He drew back the hand to inspect for tendon damage. From behind came the distinctive sounds and smells of someone losing lunch.

The cut seemed superficial if bloody. The driver was looking in all directions at once as the gypsies swirled around them, in front, to both sides, behind. "What am I going to do?" he asked.

"Drive like a motherfucker," McKay said, hauling on his machine gun again. Something told him this wasn't going to be his day.

". . . request for a produce-tithe increase of ten percent this year for farmers in the southern Oklahoma area is expected to be approved," the voice of the news announcer on KFSU droned into the fearful silence that filled the bus. "Prophet Smith offers his personal gratitude in advance to these fine believers for their generosity." One of the Blueprint people was a Mormon, who could usually be counted on to liven things up by bitching aggrievedly every time former boy-wonder television evangelist Nathan Bedford Forrest Smith, heir to the late Josiah Coffin's mantle as Prophet of the Church of the New Dispensation, was referred to as "Prophet Smith." In his current stunned state Sam couldn't even think of who it was.

He shook himself. He was in danger of slipping into combat fugue, in a way he hadn't since the very first few days after the One-Day War. Gunshots were popping off all around. The road gypsies and the Tide Camp warriors were too intermingled for either side to shoot with any degree of safety, but the bus was a great target, rising as it did above the plane of combat—and as Sloan stood there windows went popping out, one, two, three, in ringing shards of broken glass as an automatic burst raked the vehicle.

The window to the right of him was intact. He butt-stroked it out, thanking his lucky stars his rifle was a Galil with a wooden stock, instead of an American M-16 with a buttstock made by Mattel. He crouched down to fire just as another burst came right in over his head with a sound like ripping canvas.

A vehicle that seemed to have started its existence as halves of an ancient Volkswagen Bug and some kind of Japanese pickup coupled together, and gotten progressively weirder from there, was cruising right alongside, heeled over on the clay shoulder. Inside it, a man in a mask that looked to be a roughly hacked-out circle of leather with eye- and noseholes punched in it and tied to his head by a leather thong blazed away with an M-16. Sam aimed his weapon and fired. The grenade was a High-Explosive Dual-Purpose, combining the explosive force of a standard grenade with the localized armor-piercing punch of a shaped-charge warhead. He expected it to make a hell of a mess of both vehicle and occupant.

It smacked Leatherface Junior in the middle of his hairy bare chest. It knocked a hole in him the size of the Holland Tunnel, an oddly bloodless wound, and dropped him in a sprawl on top of the other nomads in the bizarre vehicle, but it didn't detonate. Sam realized with a shock that it had not completed the ten meters of free flight necessary to arm its warhead. He had choked, forgotten all about that. He had the presence of mind to spray the car with 5.56 from his Galil, however. It swerved away abruptly into the ditch and fell behind.

As the echoes of the grenade launcher's roar subsided,

the radio boomed, "We interrupt this program for a special bulletin to the faithful of America." Leering savage faces, painted like devil masks, suddenly appeared at the rear window of the bus. Gypsies were riding the bumper, trying to open the rear emergency door.

Sloan fired his Galil full automatic toward the back of the bus. One road gypsy flinched away from the shower of broken glass but held on. Sloan fired again and he disappeared without a sound. The other stuck a huge double-action revolver in the back window and fired. The metal pole rang to a hammerblow impact a few centimeters from Sloan's elbow. Desperately, Sam hosed him with gunfire. Little red measles spots appeared on the man's chest and face, blurred out in a sudden rush of blood. The horse pistol clanged to the floor of the bus as the shaven-headed gypsy disappeared from view.

"Somebody grab the gun!" Sam yelled, finding time even in the midst of this to imagine how pissed former Marine drill instructor McKay would be at his calling a pistol a *gun*. Several people scrambled for the weapon, which skittered across the floor as the bus rocked from side to side.

Dr. Connoly had insisted that the only firearms in the bus or Winnebago should be in the charge of the escorts. McKay hadn't liked that, but Sam had thought she had a point; these folks, after all, were scientists, not professional gunslingers. He was beginning to regret the decision. The bus suddenly seemed awfully large for him to defend all by himself.

"Hey," somebody called, "they're talking about us!"

". . . subversive servants of the Antichrist, including the gang of super-criminals who call themselves the Guardians, have been detected by American forces in Indiana," the KFSU radio said in the steely, fervent tones used by news announcers on fundamentalist stations.

Sloan felt his lip curl in contemptuous anger; Forrie

Smith and his people were still maintaining the fiction that the Effsee invaders constituted legitimate representatives of the American government, even though half the expeditionary force at best were Americans, and the rest were as liable to be Poles, Bulgarians, or even Soviets as anything else. A lot of folks like Reverend Forrie Smith had been impressed by the fact that the FSE expeditionary force had returned William Lowell, last elected President of the United States, to power—and just hadn't been able to see the strings that ran from the President's back straight to the blunt hand of Yevgeny Maximov.

"—but we anticipate word that the fugitives have been captured at any moment. Stay tuned—"

Somebody screamed.

Another grotesque vehicle pulled alongside with a whine of overworked engine, and an outlaw hit the side of the bus in a flying leap, his fingers locking onto the metal rim of an open window.

Sloan whirled, bringing his rifle to his shoulder. The wiry gypsy trying to force his way into the window was black, unusual for these gangs. His elaborately corn-rowed hair was dyed a shocking gold. Sloan lined up the battle sights on the center of it and gave him the standard antiterrorist double tap, two quick shots. The man went away, leaving a cupful of blood and brains dripping from the ceiling. Sloan heard retching sounds from some of the scientists hugging the floorboards.

Sloan didn't have time to pay any more attention to the radio, because here came a fresh wave of road gypsies, clinging to the side of the bus like baby opossums to their mother. He wasn't sure anyone had actually managed to recover the fallen pistol, wasn't even sure it would do any good, was acutely aware that he had no good idea how many shots remained in his thirty-five-round magazine. He looked at all those twisted faces and arms clawing in through the open windows, and figured this was just about it.

There was a bang and the bus lurched. Metal screamed on metal. The driver battled the wheel for control of the bus as the gypsies added their screams to the shriek of tortured steel. It was all over before Sloan had a clue as to what had happened: the Tide Camp battle car had sheared along the side of the bus, pulping the legs of all but two of the gypsies hanging there. Another double-tap settled one, and then Sloan heard three loud bangs from the back of the bus.

The remaining gypsy twisted frantically, clinging to a windowframe with one hand while the other came up to protect him from glass shards that peppered him as physicist Lee Warwick blazed at him with the fallen revolver. Sloan almost felt sorry for the man, but finished him off anyway.

"Better save your fire," he called back.

The physicist grinned a boyish grin. "Never was any damn good with one of these things."

Screeching, the sliding door was forced open. Sloan swung his Galil around at waist level, ready to give this intruder a faceful. At the very last micron of trigger slack Sloan's finger froze. The figure in the doorway was as outlandish as any road gypsy, with its fringed buckskin vest and warpaint, but it belonged to one of the off-center warriors from Soong's Tide Camp. "It's OK," Sloan said, waving a hand at Warwick, who was craning his horse pistol around looking for a shot. "He's on our side."

The warrior grinned, his teeth startlingly white in his paint-daubed face. "Thought you could use a hand." He brandished a pump shotgun—a Winchester Model 1897 trench gun, for God's sake, and still as good as you could get—for emphasis. He started to pull himself inside.

A yellow Honda Accord, its roof chopped off level with

the hood and the trunk lid removed to provide extra rough-and-ready passenger space, came growling in from behind. A gypsy with a crest of hair-spikes running down the center of his shaven head like some kind of exotic dinosaur stood in the backseat with his legs braced. Round and round above his head he swung a morningstar-cum-grappling hook that consisted of a coffee can that had had links of reinforcement bar sharpened at both ends hammered through it and then been filled with concrete at the end of a steel cable. His timing was flawless. The barbed weight smashed into the right side of the Tidal warrior's rib cage with such force that a spike jutted out the front of his chest. He began to topple inward, eyes wide, blood gushing from a mouth that worked like that of a beached fish. Then the cable, dogged to the car's chassis, hit the end of its slack and jerked him out of the bus in a sprawl of arms and legs, to go bouncing off down the highway behind the car like a disintegrating rag doll.

The crested gypsy stood in the back and laughed uproariously until the white phosphorous grenade from Sloan's launcher landed in the car's open trunk. The blast punched him full of pellets of metal burning with a heat to puddle steel. He stood a moment screaming, eaten alive by a hundred white-hot cancers, and then the gas tank blew and the car went doughnutting off to the right in billows of orange flame and black smoke.

Nathan Bedford Forrest Smith himself was on the radio now, called to a broadcast studio for the momentous occasion. "Smite the unbelievers hip and thigh," he thundered. "Show no mercy to the enemies of America and God!" For a boy who'd just turned thirty, he did a passing imitation of an Old Testament patriarch.

Somewhere in the bus someone began to cry uncontrollably. "We're all going to die, we're all going to die."

Sloan couldn't even tell if it was male or female.

They were probably right.

They were coming in at the windows of the Winnebago. It looked like *Night of the Living Dead* with all these clutching arms and madeup faces. Billy McKay, however, had just what it took to make even the dead lie right back down.

He finally got his machine gun and turned around. One of the administrator-types was lying still on the carpet, and another was cowering. One little sunken-chested guy was standing face-to-face with one of the outlaws, slapping at him with these ineffectual wet-noodle punches while the big gypsy just laughed and laughed. Marguerite Connoly wrestled with a couple who had her from behind and were trying to drag her out one of the blown-out windows.

"*Get down!*" McKay roared.

The cowering one stayed cowering; McKay felt contemptuous but appreciative. Belatedly the would-be featherweight champion of the Brave New World dropped like a stone, leaving his antagonist gaping down at him with a look of comic surprise. It didn't last long. The noise of the M-60 going off seemed to bulge out the thin metal walls of the Winnebago. The first burst caught the outlaw right in the chest, knocked him down and slid him clear to the rear of the vehicle. Then McKay, braced in his seat as best as he could in this peculiar ass-backward position, tucking the shock with shoulders and back and legs braced, holding the weapon by front and rear grips like the world's biggest tommy gun, twitched the barrel left and began working it clockwise, not even trying to aim, just making sure that the deadly bullet spray stayed above the prone experts.

Outlaws went everywhere. One coming in the door flew out again in a cloud of his own blood. The others were knocked off like rotten fruit out of a tree. The copper-jacketed bullets didn't even slow down going through the thin-gauge walls of the RV. By this time the badly over-loaded Winnebago was not making much speed to speak of. Half the gaudy gypsies bailed out before McKay's rav-ening chopper had a chance at them.

One of the men grappling Maggie Connoly was among the gypsies who decided to take their chances with the road bed. The other one just hitched the economist up higher with a grease-streaked bare arm around her throat and showed McKay a taunting keyboard grin. Connoly's round face was flushed with fury; her glasses were gone, her gray-shot curly hair awry. She squirmed, but lacked the strength to break away.

As the echoes of the Maremont's hysterical yammer began to subside, and the wind whistling freely through began to flush the stinks of burned powder and spilled blood and torn guts from the Winnebago, the nomad stuck the pinpoint of a commando dagger against the lobe of Connoly's left ear. "Back off, fucker," he said.

Just about that time Connoly's fingers found the little fire extinguisher set in brackets on the mock oak-paneled wall behind the john. She whipped it up and whanged the gypsy full in the face with it. He shouted, slacked his grip, scrabbled wildly to keep his precarious perch draped half-way through the window of the RV as the woman rolled off onto the floor.

McKay fired once. A single blue eye gazed out at McKay from the half of face the slug had left the gypsy, and then he slithered slowly back out of sight.

"Pretty slick, Doc," McKay said grudgingly.

Outside the road gypsies were mixing it up with the Tide Camp escorts. Less disciplined than the vets from the DC rubble, the outlaws seemed to be doing damage to their own side by cutting loose with indiscriminate bursts of au-tomatic fire into the melee. At least that's what McKay thought; he was not having all that easy a time figuring out just who was on which side. The good guys seemed to have better taste in hairdos, or at least more restraint.

Mostly the combatants were engaged in a grand high-speed combination demolition derby and street fight. Their makeshift vehicles were smashing into one another, spinning each other out or sending one another rolling across the Indiana countryside. The heavier Tide Camp vehicles got the better of most collisions, but the road gypsies' dune buggies were faster and more maneuverable. From time to time an intrepid warrior would leap from one vehicle to an enemy's and lay about with a chain, a *nunchaku*, a baseball bat with nails driven into it and the heads cut off at a bias, whatever came to hand. Other times two cars would lay alongside one another while the occupants went at it hammer and tongs, like ancient war galleys. And every now and then some Tide Camp troopie would get lucky and lob a hand grenade smack into the middle of a road gypsy car. But the outlaws had the numbers, and they were beginning to tell.

At least we know who was spotting the Effsee's artillery so badly, McKay thought as he hung his M-60 out the window of the Winnebago in hopes of getting a clear shot at some bad guys. They should have suspected it, and the KFSU broadcast Sloan was telling him about over the horn confirmed it. One of the great mysteries of life after the war was the way the Church of the New Dispensation types had hit it off with the road gypsy gangs, but they had. It was not all that uncommon for nomads and Effsees to be working together, especially here in the Midwest.

A little car like an outsized go-kart came whizzing by to starboard of the lumbering RV, right under the muzzle of McKay's Maremont. McKay triggered off a quick burst. It went high. A skinny gypsy all in black, wearing magenta insect-eye glasses, stood in back hanging on to the roll bar, laughing like a jackass and giving McKay the finger.

This could be a long day, McKay thought.

Sam Sloan watched a carload of jeering gypsies skate by not thirty meters away. He'd just popped a forty-millimeter grenade over the hood of the open Jeep and blown a chunk out of Indiana. Even at this range it hadn't been an easy shot, firing from one moving vehicle to another, but this was not a situation in which excuses counted.

He glanced back from the open door. Several of the Blueprint people were poking their heads up above the seats, peering fearfully out the windows. Sloan started to shout to them to get down, thought, *What the hell's the use?* This was finally it, for the Guardians, for the Blueprint for Renewal, for America, maybe—a sordid little backroad slaughter at the hands of scum who had dripped from society's undercarriage.

On the radio, Reverend Forrie was working himself to a fine jeremiad climax: "Let the vengeance of the Lord *strike* them *down* into destruction . . ."

Fifteen meters ahead the Jeep Sloan had missed flipped into the air. It exploded in midair, and then a curtain of earth, thrown up by a half dozen explosions, obscured it from view. After the fact Sloan's ears registered the welcome thunder of heavy automatic weapons: the guns of Mobile One.

"They're running away!" screamed a woman from a window halfway back. It was true. The skirmishing knots of vehicles and men began to disintegrate like clumps of turf thrown into a stream as the road gypsies broke off the fight and boogied.

The injured Tide Camp bus driver swayed in his seat, toppled suddenly to his right. Still holding his Galil/M-203 combo in his right hand, Sloan stopped him with his left, pushed him to slump against the side of the bus, caught the wheel, and steered the veering vehicle to the center of the cracked blacktop again. The driver's bloody lips moved briefly as if he were talking to himself, then he opened his eyes and took hold of the wheel once more.

"Oh, you saved us, thank God, you saved our lives!" sobbed the woman in the back of the bus. Sloan turned back.

"All in a day's work, ma'am. All in a day's work."

CHAPTER
THREE ―――――――――――――――――

A metronome ticking of heels followed Nathalie Frechette down the corridor, the echo-producing properties of the sterile whitewashed walls—plaster over dressed stone —making it seem that the sounds were disassociated from her, possibly possessed of a life of their own. Her head was back, jaw set, green-hazel eyes clear and bright behind the dense lenses of her glasses. She had skin of a light olive hue, the sort that turned golden on all but the briefest exposure to the sun, except she avoided sunlight. The harsh overhead lights of the tunnel turned her skin sallow, like a corpse's, sunk her eyes in ashy pits, and lent her dark orange hair an unreal, metallic sheen. Her tautly erect posture conspired to counteract the effect of her dress, which seemed calculated to hide her full, firm figure. Today she had on a baggy blouse of a grayish color one couldn't quite pin down, a wool skirt of a murky greenish plaid reminiscent of something a Catholic schoolgirl might wear. Her heels, though low, made that tick-tick-ticking sound that followed her like a shadow.

Schloss Ehrenbreitstein had enjoyed a long and checkered history. Its position on a great sheer cliff overlooking the city of Koblenz on the confluence of the Rhine and Neckar rivers lent it some strategic importance. It had undergone several incarnations as a castle, been destroyed on a couple of occasions. It had been a *Wehrmacht* command post during the Second World War—old walls standing among weeds on the clifftop still bore bulletholes in the unmistakable stitchlike pattern of automatic-weapons fire. It had become a youth hostel after that war, and enjoyed a final, brief fling as a NATO command post during the week of ground fighting that was the prelude to the One-Day War.

Now it was the capital of Europe.

The corridor was a succession of featureless metal doors painted a dusty green. The air lay in a dead mass periodically stirred by breaths from ventilation ducts. It had that smell that cried *Institution*, compromising a bit more than the usual mildew and a bit more than the usual disinfectant, with the mucous membrane–drying tang of air conditioning and just a hint of cavern cool. Nathalie went to a door indistinguishable from the others, opened it without knocking.

A billow of steam hit her in the face like an enormous feather pillow. She hesitated, choking on a sudden humidity. "For the good God's sake, come in and shut the door," boomed the voice of her lord and master from somewhere in all that fog.

Flushing angrily, she did as she was bid. She stepped forward, heels ticking irritably on the tile floor, and suddenly the fog parted and there he was, lying on his hairy paunch having his back pummeled by an enormously muscled Negro wearing only purple satin trunks.

Yevgeny Maximov was built like a bear. He had broad, flat feet, short, almost bandy legs. His body had the dimensions of an oil drum, the arms thick as light poles, though showing little muscular definition. For all the years of soft living he had known as a world-class financier and man of mystery, Maximov's body had made few concessions to late middle age. There was very little of softness to him.

He raised his massive head. Insinuating fingers of steam had pried up a few tufts of dark hair customarily slicked back along the broad skull, returning it to its native bushiness. He was balding on top, a fact he characteristically disdained to conceal. He never concealed anything of his person or personality; that was a defense mechanism, and that meant weakness. His designs, of course, were another matter—or at least, had been until the One-Day War gave him the opportunity to openly assert his mastery of Europe.

Maximov's face was heavy, the eyes small and dark, the nose shapeless from frequent breakage, a memento of youth spent under circumstances far removed from his present luxury. His beard was thick and full and shot with gray. His lips were thick, had a slightly purple tinge.

The lips broke into a smile. "Ah, Nathalie, you've come to brighten my morning, I trust? That's enough for now, Jean-Jacques." The black left off the meat-tenderizing treatment with his mighty hands and stepped back.

Nathalie looked uneasily away. Maximov frowned. "What's this? Don't tell me you disturbed my massage to bring me bad news?" Frowning massively, he studied her an instant longer, then the frown subsided back into the normal cragginess of his face. "Aha. I see. The presence of nearly naked men disturbs you. One might almost think you were still a virgin, *hein?*"

Nathalie flushed furious maroon. "That's none of your business!" she flashed, her eyes still avoiding both the vast body lying on the padded bench, covered only with a towel across the rump, and the squat, sweating black man.

The response of the most powerful man on earth to this insufferable impertinence was a chuckle that seemed to rumble up from the center of the earth. "Ah, *ma petite,* but you make it too simple to keep you off-balance. Come, give me the good news, since I perceive that's what you bring me."

She drew in a deep breath, sharply to the edge of gasping. How well he read her. Had she not believed so wholeheartedly in what she perceived as his plan to save the world by unifying it under his firm, just guidance, she might have thought him a devil. She made her eyes meet his.

"Mr. Chairman, you may recall that in the very last days preceding the destruction of Heartland Complex by the Guardians and their bandit allies, our technicians had finally succeeded in gaining access to the computer files containing all data the Americans had assembled concerning the Blueprint for Renewal."

A heavy nod. "That minor detail failed to escape me."

The sarcasm made her falter briefly, then, "They, ah, that is to say our agents in North America, were able to transmit a substantial portion of the Blueprint data to us via satellite relays." Wonderful things, satellites; most of them had survived the war, despite efforts by the Soviets to knock them out. By the mid 1990s, there were simply too many in operation to effectively blitz the West's communications. So a good number of them functioned on, impervious to the war and to the turmoil that had followed it alike.

"We were able to synthesize this information with data procured for us prior to the war by our contacts in the American government infrastructure, notably your late viceroy, Trajan. By this means we have made a momentous discovery—more correctly, uncovered what may have been a momentous discovery by the North Americans. Perhaps the single most vital element of the Blueprint for Renewal," she finished breathlessly.

The bushy eyebrows swept up. The shaggy, recumbent body seemed to swell with a tension Frechette had never seen in Maximov before, not even when he learned that his most trusted operative, Nathalie's own predecessor as his chief aide, lay near death after almost being assassinated by one of the Guardians. "Well? What is it, then?"

"On-line fusion power."

He stared at her a moment, eyes radiating black heat. A jerk of the head: "Jean-Jacques, leave us. *Now.*" The black departed as silently as a coil of the now-dissipating mist.

He shut his eyes for a moment, then opened them again and looked at her. "By the way you are hopping from foot to foot like a schoolgirl asking to be excused for a pee, I infer you cannot wait to ask me if I realize what this implies?"

As intended, the vulgarity made her flush, but she nodded valiantly.

"Well, child, listen to an old man and see if he misses anything. On-line fusion power would open up a source of energy potentially greater by orders of magnitude than any hitherto available. To all practical intents unlimited."

She nodded eagerly. "Yes, Excellency, yes."

"If this is true," he said, eyes half-lidded and unfocused, apparently to himself, "then truly it is the ultimate secret of the Blueprint for Renewal. With a fusion reactor in my possession, the rest of the Blueprint—all the wealth of America, in fact—is so much dross. With this—"

He held up one hand balled into a huge hairy fist. "With it, I would hold the entire world"—the hand unfolded—"here."

CHAPTER
FOUR ──────────────────────────

The air hummed faintly with air conditioning in the briefing room in the newly reopened West Wing of the White House. Up front, Carrie Andrews, a pinched unhappy-looking computer expert in her mid-thirties, brushed absently with a hand at pale, dry hair and leafed nervously through several folders and stacks of printouts. She had on a ribbed white sleeveless blouse with the stretch long since washed out of it, and baggy salmon-colored shorts. Waiting for his assistant to marshal her sources, physicist Lee Warwick doodled on the blackboard with a wet-chalk marker. He was doing a cartoon of an anthropomorphized mouse with big round Mickey ears and a long, toothy rat's leer. It was quite a good cartoon. Warwick was dressed in inordinately baggy khaki shorts and a horrible mostly blue aloha shirt that forcibly reminded Sam Sloan of how much he didn't miss the eighties.

The physicist added a few finishing touches to the rat. It seemed to be dressed the same way he was, gazing back at his creator with a knowingly cynical uplift of an eyebrow. "Are you ready, Carrie?" the physicist asked.

The young woman had flipped open a battery-powered notebook computer on the table at the front of the room, was punching buttons and frowning at the liquid-crystal display. She nodded.

"Well, I must say I feel a bit self-conscious. It's not often I get to lecture such a high-powered audience—the Guardians, the President of the United States." A quick-silver grin. "At least I don't have to worry about anyone dozing off while I lecture. Unless Morpheus has already got Lieutenant Wilson, there, in his clutches."

He nodded toward the far end of the briefing chamber, where Casey was laid out in a chair with his combat boots up on the table and a Rolling Stones concert cap tipped low over his nose. "I'm, like, listening, Professor," he stammered.

Sitting back in a padded plastic chair and crossing his randy legs, Sam Sloan smiled. "Don't mind him, Doc. Casey's got two modes: hyper and comatose."

Warwick grinned. His assistant muttered something uneasily. "All right. We'd better get on with this before Maggie gets on my case. She gets ants in her pants at the thought of anything interfering with her great work of reconstruction."

Into a moment of uncomfortable silence, President MacGregor said, "That's all right, Professor. I'll take care of keeping Dr. Connolly mollified." He was the one the former Harvard economist was most annoyed with, for taking time away from the *de facto* cabinet the Guardians had retrieved from Luxor—though what she was *most* worked up about was the circumstances attending the briefing.

The physicist nodded. "Thanks, Mr. President. Carrie?"

As if reluctantly, the young woman looked up from her computer screen. She cleared her throat and said, "As we already told you gentlemen, two hours ago our personnel monitoring radio traffic received a broadcast on a special channel set aside especially for the use of the Guardians. At first we considered this an anomaly, until we ascertained that the signal was being relayed through one of the communications satellites that still survive in orbit. It was *directed* here.

"The parties originating the communication utterly refused to talk to anyone who was not one of the Guardians." *Which ticked Maggie off royally,* Sloan thought with wry amusement. "Fortunately, once we were able to get Commander Sloan on the line and establish his bona fides, the call's originators were able to provide us with information which, if true, could prove to be of the greatest moment."

Everybody looked at Sloan. "Awright, what's the big secret?" McKay demanded.

"It was our friends in Freehold," Sloan said. "With the codes we gave them from the computer of the FSE vehicle which became our current Mobile One, they still own Eff-see communications, no matter what they do to try to secure them. Using the satellite and data-link relays, they can even get into their European complex to a limited extent. It takes your breath away." He shook his head appreciatively. "Anyway, they're mainly working with the underground Dr. Morgenstern has got working against Maitland's FSE military government in California, but it seems they've stumbled onto something big."

"So what the fuck is it?" McKay rasped, pulling a half-smoked stub of cigar out of the breast pocket of his silver-gray coveralls. The computer expert flushed at his language. He leered at her.

"First off, they managed to confirm what we've been

afraid of: the Effsees were able to crack open the Blueprint data base before the major blew Heartland."

The other Guardians nodded. "The people at Freehold have been passing on enough stuff to make that pretty clear, man," Casey remarked.

"It's our best guess, and Dr. Andrews"—he nodded at the woman—"and the other computer specialists among recovered Blueprint personnel concur, that they were only able to obtain the information we had amassed on Project Blueprint, including data of little current application, such as the location of personnel whom we've already recovered. However, our esteemed friend Chairman Maximov has had access to a good many more trained personnel with a lot more time to go over this information than we have since the fall of Heartland."

McKay took the unlit cigar out from between his jaws. "Yeah. We been preoccupied with a few little details like gettin' the President to safety and then recapturing Washington, DC."

"Sam," the President said gently, "you are about to come to some point, aren't you?"

"Of course, Mr. President. It appears that the FSE analysts may have found information that points to what our friends in the Freehold, with Dr. Morgenstern's agreement, call the ultimate secret of Project Blueprint."

"So what the hell is it already?" bellowed McKay.

"On-line fusion power."

A moment's stunned silence greeted the words. Then: "Far *out!*" exclaimed Casey, and the President said, "My God," and even Tom Rogers's stone face raised its eyebrows.

At once MacGregor sobered. "If this is true, this could be the greatest boon imaginable, not just for America, but for all mankind. Yet forgive me if I'm skeptical, Commander Sloan. There have been so many expansive claims made for the glories of fusion power—as there were for nuclear energy before them—as well as so many predictions of an imminent breakthrough in the fusion field that somehow just didn't pan out."

Frowning, McKay studied the cigar as if suspecting somebody'd slipped him a dog turd wrapped in a tobacco leaf. "So what's the big deal with this fusion stuff, anyway?"

Sam nodded to Warwick and Carrie Andrews. "That's in their line. Once I convinced Angie it was me, I turned her over to those two to hash out the highbrow stuff." Angie was Angelina Connoly, perhaps the closest thing to a leader the anarchists of Freehold acknowledged. She was also the daughter of Dr. Marguerite Connoly, *de facto* chief of the White House staff and the second most powerful person in America. To round it off, she was also more than just a good friend to Casey Wilson, to whom she'd sent her love. There had been no such greeting for her mother; in fact Angie had never spoken her last name.

"Commander Sloan's shitkicker modesty is getting the better of him." Sam's eyebrows snapped up; Casey stifled a snicker, and McKay made no attempt to hide his malicious grin. For somebody as apparently easygoing as Warwick was, the physicist could be surprisingly blunt at times. Almost rude. "He was quite competent to follow the conversation, though the real meat of the matter came in the form of a data transmission Carrie captured for us, and is just itching to get back to. But I appreciate the commander's deferring to me; gives me a chance to look like I'm earning my keep."

Readjusting his grip on his marker, which he'd been twirling over and over between thumb and forefinger, he stepped back to the blackboard. "Just so everyone knows what we're talking about: nuclear energy—the stuff used to make the power plants run, and gave the Hiroshima and

Nagasaki bombs their punch—involves splitting up the nuclei of big, heavy, unstable atoms. It's not that difficult a process to get going, but it's expensive, and tricky to deal with, of course. They're radioactive—"

"Yeah, I remember when that plant went up back in Russia, and they started making us shut down all the ones over here 'cause they were afraid of the same thing happening," McKay commented.

"On the other hand," Warwick said, "*fusion* reactions have a lot of advantages over fission ones. The materials they require are fairly cheap, for one thing. What fuses is hydrogen, after all, and that's everywhere around us, mostly in the form of water. Also, the end product of fusion is helium, which is not only not radioactive, but a fairly useful little gas, so that we do away with a lot of the problems of waste disposal posed by nuclear power."

Warwick stopped and looked at his audience. Even this brief monologue had been enough to make McKay scrunch up in his chair with his arms crossed and his massive chin tucked right in against his chest.

"Are you following me, Lieutenant McKay?" the physicist asked. McKay produced a sound like a gigantic toad being stepped on. The physicist grinned.

"Your fearless leader obviously would prefer if I kept this lecture brief, so I'll try to oblige him.

"Anyway, another point is the *efficiency* of nuclear fusion. Certain kinds of fusion produce your electricity directly, instead of having to heat water to make steam to drive turbines to make generators go 'round, the way nuclear-fission plants work. This gives you a tremendous increase in efficiency.

"When you combine that with the low cost and a much greater safety factor, you have something pretty nifty."

McKay took the cigar out of his mouth again. "Great. What's all this got to do with us?"

"Everything."

"Project Starshine," the President said.

Everybody looked at him. "We were building it, as part of Project Blueprint," MacGregor expanded. "Crenna briefed me on it back in Heartland, before . . . before the troubles."

"But what Warwick is talking about is years away!" Sam exclaimed.

The President looked to the physicist. "Starshine had achieved break-even eight months before the war," Warwick said with a smirk. "At the rate at which they were progressing, they would probably be able to produce an energy surplus—usable power—by now. Provided that the facility survived. And there's every reason to believe that it has."

"But—but why didn't Major Crenna say anything to us about this?" Sam demanded.

"Security, Sam," Rogers said in his bland drawl. "What we didn't know, we couldn't spill, either by accident or if we got captured."

"But surely, there wouldn't be any harm in people knowing something like this existed—"

"Sure there is," McKay mumbled. "If the bad guys caught one word of this 'Starshine' stuff, they'd go bug-fuck trying to get their hands on it. The rest of the Blueprint equals squat, compared to something like this."

A little chagrined, Sloan nodded. Once again he was reminded McKay hadn't been made leader of the Guardians through bureaucratic oversight. He may have been big enough and ugly enough to make Rambo cry for his mommy, but he was a long way from stupid.

"Only now the bad guys know it exists . . . and know where it is."

"Not exactly," quiet Carrie said.

"The good news is," Warwick said, "that aside from the fact that it's located somewhere in southern Louisiana, the

Federated States of Europe have no idea of where the Project Starshine facility is."

Sloan nodded. "And the bad news?"

"Neither do we."

CHAPTER
FIVE ———————————————

"Tanks," Colonel Enos Correy said, standing on the flying bridge of the troopship FSS *General Marshall*. He shook his gray, close-cropped head. "One hell of a lot of good they're going to do us in *that*."

He nodded his Kirk Douglas crag of a chin at the gently waving reeds of the Louisiana marshlands fringing Terrebonne Bay a hundred and forty kilometers west of the mouth of the Mississippi.

"But, Colonel, won't their firepower come in handy if the locals are intransigent?" asked his youthful aide, Captain Mancuso, glancing at the Landing Ship, Tank *Newport* riding like a gray cardboard box at anchor two hundred meters off their starboard beam. A head taller than his commanding officer, Mancuso displayed the rangy exuberance of a bluetick pup and a handsomeness that would have been called clean-cut except for the ever-present shadow on his cheeks, totally razor-resistant, caused by the blue-blackness of his hair and beard. With his sharp blue eyes and eyebrows like swatches of lampblack, he could have been a 1950's leading man, if you beefed him up a bit.

Correy laughed without amusement. "We know—or hope we know—that the secret facility's somewhere on this coast between the Mississippi and Texas. That leaves almost five hundred kilometers of coast to play in—with scarcely a square meter of reliably solid ground for klicks inland. Hell, in a lot of this country, the word coastline doesn't mean a damn thing. Terrain goes from marsh to swamp to bayou. The only place you can run the damn tanks is on the roads—where the causeways haven't washed out. If we run into any opposition at all worth the name, the things'll be deathtraps."

Mancuso looked about nervously. "Don't let Political Officer Myers hear you say that, sir. Our TO&E was approved by the Chairman himself."

"Maybe. And maybe some paper-pusher in Rotterdam had some spare tracks he wanted off his inventory. Or who knows what. Just because the FSE is bringing necessary order to Europe and the United States doesn't mean every last one of its damned bureaucrats is an angel."

"Sir—" Mancuso shut up and squinted off across the gray-green water toward a black line of cypress and palmetto visible beyond the reeds that marked the land's ostensible beginning. Though the day was overcast, the heaving water still tossed up eye-hurting lints of glare like bits of broken glass.

The youthful captain was acutely uncomfortable. Enos Correy was a genuine American patriot. The blue-and-white FSE badge sewed to the shoulder of his uniform in no way diminished that fact. He believed with his heart and soul that the Federated States of Europe was the key to restoring order—and greatness—to the land of his birth and first allegiance. Though a young man, by no means the seasoned campaigner the diminutive, scar-faced colonel was, Mancuso had spent some time with FSE Defense Force Supreme Headquarters before being attached to this special-mission group. He had a better grasp of the political realities inside the Federation. Or at least, he was afraid he did.

"What about the air-cushion vehicles?" he asked, a bit too eagerly, trying gently to prod his superior into making comments that might be more favorably interpreted by any overhearing ears.

To his dismay Correy snorted. "They tried the damn things in 'Nam. Didn't work any too well there. Too damn vulnerable and noisy. Always breaking down."

"But, sir! That was thirty years ago. Hovercraft technology's improved since then."

Correy shrugged. "Maybe. If the beasts work, they could be handy at that. Damn sight better than tanks, anyway."

The colonel turned his face from a breeze heavy with the scent of moist vegetation and the stink of fuel oil. As if by coincidence, a tall, rail-thin figure stepped from the shadowed interior of the bridge. Correy nodded briskly to Political Officer Myers. The PO showed white teeth in a smile.

"Afternoon, Colonel. Are we about ready to begin debarcation?"

Contact with the indifferent daylight was already turning the lenses of his horn-rimmed glasses dark, so that his eyes seemed to be vanishing slowly into dark-gray fogbanks. Correy looked away as if the sight unnerved him.

"We got a scouting party inshore, providing always they can *find* a shore. We want to wait to commit ourselves until we're sure what kind of reception we'll get—if any, that is." His lips twisted in a joyless gesture that resembled a smile.

Myers showed a quick flash of ivory again. "Good judgment, Colonel." His brow furrowed under a shock of pallid straw-dry Andy Warhol hair bobbing gently in the breeze as he gazed off at the black cypress. "I only hope we're far enough from New Orleans," he said, his voice edged with concern.

"Oh, sir, it's nothing to worry about. The fallout's died back long since. Just to make sure, Captain Huysmann's people have been testing the wind and water; radiation's within the limits of what our computers tell us to expect from background in these parts," said Mancuso.

"I think the political officer is talking about plague, Francis," the colonel said.

The PO nodded vigorously. "Our intelligence indicates the New Orleans and Baton Rouge areas were hit hard by a number of epidemics, including some we haven't been able to identify."

"Yeah. Well, we sure-hell haven't see any sign of life on this coast. In a way that's a blessing, much as I hate to say it. Fewer people we run into hereabouts, the less chance of contagion." Mancuso looked narrowly at the former CIA operative. "This is where our orders said to establish a beachhead, after all. Roughly midpoint of the projected search area."

"Of course, of course," said Myers.

A young man with a prominent Adam's apple and white Royal Navy uniform displaying the ubiquitous FSE shoulderpatch emerged from the bridge. "Captain's compliments, Colonel, and he wishes to report we've heard from one of our recce parties," he said, saluting snappily.

Correy returned the gesture with a sharpness that snapped his cuff like a whip. "What did they say?"

"The town marked on our maps as Cocodrie appears to be inhabited, sir." He glanced up at the sky, which was clotting with darker clouds. The breeze was freshening. "They also report seeing signs of heavy storm damage in the settlement, sir."

Correy nodded dismissively. "I suppose we should send a party inshore to talk to the locals. I'd be relieved if we could start landing people at once. My men have just about forgotten what it's like *not* to be seasick. All right, Francis, get on the horn to *Newport*—"

"Begging the Colonel's pardon, sir," said the ensign, his Adam's apple bobbing.

Correy raised his shaggy brows. "What is it, son?"

"There seems to be rather a nasty bit of weather brewing up, sir. And this *is* the hurricane season, sir," the British ensign said.

"You're saying you think we ought to delay landing?" The boy faced him, but his eyes sidled ever so slightly toward the gangling PO. Correy wasn't having any. "Well?" he prodded.

"Er, yes. Yes, sir."

"Damn. I wish we still had reliable satellite weather coverage. Well, I guess we had better forget about landing just now." He jerked his head aft toward Wind Island, an all-but-submerged mass lying across the bay's mouth. "Will that be enough to protect us if a storm blows up?"

"Should do, sir. It will help, anyway." The youthful officer looked relieved.

"Very well. Recall the reconnaissance craft." Correy turned away. His hands gripped the chipped paint of the railing.

"I have a feeling," he said into the rising wind, "this is going to be one hell of a mission."

• • •

The storm was coming fast. Already it was reaching out over the bayous with fingers of wind-whipped rain, and the clouds raced overhead like fiercely driven horses. The chunky white vessel, bristling with antennas and armaments, raising a sweeping mustache of froth at its prow as it smashed through waves just beginning to show white crests, was fleeing. But not from the approaching storm.

Patrol Boat *461*, seventy-five feet over the waterline, was armed with two double twenty-millimeter quick-firing cannon turrets, torpedo tubes mounted amidships to either side of the superstructure, and up front a turret mounting a twenty-millimeter Gatling gun, radar-aimed, devastating against targets both on the surface and in the air. She had been a vessel of the United States Coast Guard, but no American flag cracked from her mast in the breeze of her passage. Perhaps from shame.

Even in the days before the One-Day War, the temptations involved in the U.S. war on drugs had proven overwhelming for some members of the Coast Guard. A really sizable drug bust could provide a haul plenty big enough to win praises and promotions from superiors, and still leave more than enough to hold back to sell for *beaucoup* bucks on the street. Since anybody connected in any way, shape, or form with drug enforcement who sported an IQ in two figures knew damn well what tended to happen to confiscated drugs, it was easy enough to see that as merely getting your share before the higher-ups cashed in.

The captain and crew of *461* had been among those who gave in to temptation. They had found life since the One-Day War most congenial. They were, as they never failed to inform those who fell prey to them, loyally enforcing the customs and immigrations laws of the United States of America. The fact that the U.S. of A. was, as far as they could ascertain, defunct merely meant they didn't have to split their take with anyone anymore.

But now 461's time was running out. The torpedo tubes in her waist stood empty, memento of a confrontation with a cutter manned by former Coast Guard comrades who had not been so uninhibitedly ready to embrace the New Order. And against the nemesis which stalked her, 461's guns were as useless as peashooters.

In open water she could have outrun the hunter. But bad fortune had trapped the quarry between the stalker and the shore. The only hope had been to make use of her better speed to sprint inshore, trusting to the rain squalls to conceal her until she could find shelter in one of the black bayous that writhed into the bay like snakes, or up the mighty Atchafalaya River itself. Once up a bayou, the predator with her greater draft would never catch her, nor could her radars seek her out amid the tangles of hummocks and cypress trees.

The gamble seemed to be working. 461's radar showed the predator still out in the Gulf, beyond North Point, a good ten klicks away. Just a few thousand more meters—

It came out of a squall, stark white against gunmetal water and sky, strangely silent, three meters above the tossing whitecaps. Sixteen feet long, an extended arrowhead, seeking its prey with a single radar eye as it flashed forward at better than ninety percent of the speed of sound. The captain of 461 barely had time to react to the lookout's warning; the missile never produced so much as a flicker on her radar screens.

With commendable quickness of reflexes the helmsman put the wheel all the way over to port. The fleeing vessel hadn't deviated three degrees from her course when the ship-killer smashed through the taffrail, plunged through the deck at the root of the Z-turret twin twenty mike-mike and on into the central stores locker amidships before detonating.

In the Falklands War of a decade and a half before, a missile of the type on which this one was modeled had sunk a British warship fifty times *461*'s size, and debate still raged as to whether it had even gone off. There would, however, be no question about the explosion of the three hundred and fifty pounds of high explosive in *this* warhead.

The middle section of the patrol boat simply vanished in a giant orange fireball. And that was that.

The secondary explosions of fuel and munitions had finally stopped, but the floating bow and stern sections of the stricken boat were still burning thirty minutes later when a sheet of rain parted like a theatrical curtain to reveal her killer stalking into the bay to examine its kill. Four hundred and five feet long, gray as a blade, shaped like a knife seen in section: the *Cienfuegos,* last surviving ship of the Cuban navy, the turbines of her two cruising engines growling hungrily.

Three men emerged from the bridge at the forward rail next to the instrument shack. The man in the center raised a pair of heavy binoculars to his eyes and surveyed the burning wreck.

"We should put a boat over and look for survivors," said the taller, slimmer man on his right, who wore a rainslick and a naval officer's cap that just barely kept sporadic rain off his lordly prominence of nose. He had a vandyke beard and a mustache with waxed tips.

"Don't listen to him, Captain Asusta," growled the short, bandy-legged man who stood to the other side of the man with the binoculars. He had the black beret and jungle camouflage smock of a Marine, with web gear belted over the smock and a heavy American-made .45 hanging from it in a flapped holster. He was furiously bearded. "I say unlimber a machine gun, in case any of the imperialists escaped."

The man in the middle lowered his binoculars. He was on the tall side, a bit short of six feet, with high, wide cheekbones and an athletic build. His dark hair was medium length and swept neatly back beneath his own officer's cap, his beard trimmed short. He took a slim cigar from the pocket of his khaki shirt, bit the end off, delicately spat it out, put it in his mouth and lit it with a flick of a disposable lighter. "We'll do neither. Lieutenant Cardenas"—he glanced at his lanky executive officer—"we lack the facilities to accommodate prisoners, in particular wounded ones. As for your suggestion, Sergeant Maestre, we're not barbarians. Should any crew have survived the explosion of our missile, more power to them; I'll not add to their misery. If they make it to shore alive, they deserve to. But they will do so without any help from us." He drew on the cigar, released a plume of smoke that looked light against the gray day.

The tall man said something under his breath. The captain raised an eyebrow. "I beg your pardon, Comrade Cardenas?"

The exec looked down at the raindrops bouncing off the immaculately shined toes of his shoes. "I said this looks like a pestilential coast, Captain."

"We need to make repairs, Lieutenant. This bay appears to offer the chance to do so with a minimal chance of interruption. To say nothing of the opportunity to get off this damned ship for a few hours."

The stocky sergeant emitted a derisive snort. "The comrade lieutenant is afraid to scuff his shoes. Well, don't worry; my Guard Flotilla boys will handle things ashore.

You can sit inside where it's dry and watch your instruments and screens."

Cardenas sent him a look that sizzled like a firebrand dropped in water. The sergeant gazed coolly back as if daring the taller man to make something of it. Asusta shook his head.

"Gentlemen," he said reprovingly, "this is no way to talk. We've got to show solidarity if we're going to embark on the liberation of the former United States of America." And he laughed at their expressions.

CHAPTER
SIX ─────────────────────────

"Shit," Billy McKay said as a drop of gummy rain hit him in the left eyelid. "This is gonna be so much fun I can just barely stand to think about it."

Pinging and cooling beneath a sky the same color as its armored hull, Mobile One sat parked at a former Fina station beside a blacktop road somewhere south of the ruins of Baton Rouge, not far from the fringes of the sprawling Atchafalaya Basin swamp. Back road though this was, it was still strung like a black string with the misshapen beads of cars—or husks of cars—corroded and rusted from a year's exposure to the unremitting rains of the Southern coast. Though the area surrounding the former state capital had been fairly heavily reclaimed and developed, a lot of it hadn't seemed to take; for some kilometers already the only reliable land had all too often been the bed of the road itself. During the last hour and a half, Mobile

One had been crawling along with its wheels angled on a road embankment made up of crushed clamshells, so that the vehicle was covered in a fine coat of chalky dust. Its occupants had gratefully piled out to stand for a few moments on level, if not particularly firm, ground.

"I feel as if I should be standing tipped to the left," remarked Sam Sloan, pacing back and forth in front of gas pumps like lonely decommissioned robots, their LCD displays staring like dull empty eyes, taking knee-raising steps and twisting his neck left and right to loosen it. "My semicircular canals keep telling me that's the only way to stay upright."

McKay yawned like a zoo lion at midday, put his close-cropped head back and stretched, making the muscles on his bare back writhe. Another fat raindrop hit him on the forehead. He wiped it away with a quick motion. "Jesus. That stuff feels like birdcrap."

"Welcome to bayou country, Billy," said Rogers, sitting in the open hatch of the turret. Like the other three Guardians, he had doffed his shirt. McKay squinted up at him, eyebrows fisting, suspecting him of being facetious. But, no, the stocky former Green Beret just sat up there looking as calm and serious as he always did.

"That's easy for *you* to say," McKay said in disgust. "*I* didn't spend my field time running around the goddamnedest swamps in Southeast Asia and Central goddam America."

"I was mostly in the highlands in Asia," replied Rogers, imperturbable as always.

A grizzled old black man, wearing denim overalls over a white T-shirt, came stomping around the corner of the cinderblock building, carrying three bottles of soda, glistening from the water of the stream that rolled, green and rain-gravid, behind the station, with their necks trapped between the fingers of his huge hands. His clothes and craggy features had a slightly ashy look to them, as if the white dust of the roadbed had been ground into them by time.

"Sorry I don't got no gas'line for you boys," he said in a voice thick and slow as highway tar. "But I had the kind of pop you wanted. It ain't too cold, but I can't afford to buy ice. Creek keeps it kind of cool, anyway." He held all three bottles dangling from one hand while he unreeled his cable keychain from its silver spool at his waist, popped the tops with a church key.

"Thanks, man," Casey said, accepting a tepid bottle of Nehi orange soda. He was sitting on the front glacis of the vehicle with his bootheels braced against the steel-bar cages that enclosed the headlights. He passed a bottle of brown fluid up to Tom while the old man handed another of the same to Sloan.

The old guy turned to McKay. "What was you wantin', d'you decide, sir?"

"Beer."

The old man's brow creased in consternation. He shook his head. "No, no, I done told you, sir, I ain't got none of that. I serve any of that alcohol, reg'lators come and shut me down good. I only got this here soda pop. What kind would you like? It's nice and refreshing, on a day like this, even if it ain't none too cool."

Sloan held up his bottle. "Try some of this Barq's root beer, McKay. This is the part of the country where it comes from. It's pretty good."

"I never drank that stuff. The way they write the name on the label, it looks too much like 'Barf's.' And the way it looks, it coulda just been scooped up out of that sewer back there."

He turned back to the old man, standing patiently by wiping his hands on a rag from his back pocket. "All right. I want a Coke."

"Diet, no-caffeine, or reg'lar?"

McKay blinked. "Regular."

"New Coke or Classic Coke?"

"Jesus *Christ!*" McKay roared. "Old Coke, with caffeine and sugar and all that other good shit. The new stuff tastes too much like Pepsi, anyway."

The old man started to shuffle back to the stream. "Say, sir, like, excuse me," Casey called. "Where do you get this stuff, anyway?" He brandished a half-empty bottle of orange soda.

"I buys salvage out of Baton Rouge." He ambled off toward the stream.

McKay crossed his arms and leaned back against the side of Mobile One's angular snout. "How's the hand, McKay?" Sloan asked, still pacing back and forth to work the kinks out of his legs. He was a runner, and being confined in the steel womb of Mobile One for long hours really got to him. The close confines did, anyway—he was a deepwater Navy man, who had distinguished himself in a fight in the Sidra Gulf aboard the cruiser *Winston-Salem,* and alone among the Guardians was accustomed to going into battle surrounded by armor plating.

McKay's ice-blue eyes flickered reflexively toward the tape wrapping the knuckles of his huge right hand. "Fine, thanks, and fuck you too, sailor." Sloan laughed.

For the Guardians more than any other troop, even soldiers in a combat zone, life was a weird, erratic seesaw between tension and tedium. Each man's war record, as well as an exhaustive battery of psychological tests—which they all suspected the shadowy Major Crenna hadn't put much stock in anyway—had established that each man was that rare specimen, the one warrior in a million or more who actually thrived on the stresses of combat.

Most soldiers could bear the constant strains of a war zone only for weeks at a time, and a stretch of, say, six months unbroken would make a man unfit for service as surely as paralysis. But from the duties envisioned for the Guardians at the moment of the team's inception, there would be no rotation home, no relief or reinforcements. And no foreseeable end to the tour of duty. The Guardians would have to get by under conditions that would normally be expected to produce a psychological casualty rate of a flat one hundred percent. That was one reason why out of the millions of men and women in America's armed services, only four had measured up as Guardians.

That didn't mean they always had to like their circumstances. They were iron men, each in his own way, but the unending emotional and physical pressure in the field wore them down. And then the downtime, like the last few weeks in mostly pacified Washington, made them restless and edgy as caged predators. The routine would have snapped lesser men. Even the Guardians sometimes showed the strains.

The night before they'd left on this little pleasure cruise, Tide Camp and the rest of their allies in the rubble had thrown a going-away blowout for the Guardians. During the course of the celebration McKay had gotten shitfaced on scarfed—salvaged—beer and, reverting to the form of his uproarious youth, gotten into a fight. The good news was that, instead of picking on one of their none-too-certain allies, the former Marine had chosen to duke it out with one of the cement-and-steel lampposts looming on the Mall. The bad news was, the lamppost won.

The top-ranked physicians among the Blueprint crew, and team medic Tom Rogers—whose opinion McKay trusted above that of any highbrow, anyway—had all agreed the bones weren't broken, but he sure hadn't done his hand a hell of a lot of good. It had been a damn-fool thing to do right before a mission, but these men were his buddies, his comrades, a team closer than most married couples, who had been through the fires of hell together.

Naturally, they gave him rafts of shit.

"This place stinks," McKay growled, shaking his head. "This whole thing stinks."

The air carried a lush greenness that was alien, almost obscene to city-boy nostrils raised on a diet of hot concrete and diesel fumes and steel-mill smoke. There was also the smell of brackish water, from the little green-scum stream and the cypress forests that seemed to loom like ramparts, never far away, mysterious and forbidding.

There was more: the smell of death. The bodies of millions killed by the bombing of New Orleans and Baton Rouge, and the terrible plagues that followed, had rotted to nothing months before in the vast wet greenhouse heat. But still somehow the stink lingered, slightly sweet, a trace like a memory of nightmare. Old soldiers Rogers and McKay knew that smell from long ago; Casey and Sam, who had fought a cleaner, more impersonal sort of war, hadn't known it as their constant companion throughout their military careers. But they too had become conversant with the smell of death, in the charnel pits that the One-Day War had made of the cities of America.

"At least the plague's died down," Casey remarked, as if reading McKay's mind.

"We hope," McKay said darkly.

"Oh, it has, Billy," Rogers said reassuringly. "Population's thinned down enough hereabouts, wouldn't support any major epidemic."

"You can't imagine how comforting that is."

Sam had stopped pacing and begun doing stretching exercises. "But we can't even be sure of that, Tom. What we've got in the way of hard intelligence we stole from the FSE. And *they* don't know a heck of a lot."

Rogers had nothing to say to that, so he shrugged. He was not a man to speak unless he had something pressing to be said. The vehicle was stocked with the most up-to-date medical paraphernalia, prewar edition: a computerized diagnostic kit that would fit into a suitcase, broad-spectrum antibiotics, monoclonal antibodies gene-tailored to attack the pathogens the Guardians seemed most likely to encounter. They'd trust to that, Tom's savvy, and their brute animal health. It was a combination that had kept them alive so far.

"It's times like this that I really miss Major Crenna," Casey said, taking a long pull at his Nehi.

"You took the words right out of my mouth," McKay grumbled.

Previously, when they were sent out on a mission, they'd had the benefit of intelligence, sketchy but generally accurate, gleaned from a continent-spanning network whose real extent not even the Guardians had been fully able to fathom; a full briefing on conditions on the ground, an idea of what if any assets the Guardians could hope to find near their objective. It wasn't as if they'd ever been provided with a lot of data or a lot of help; Crenna wasn't a superman, though as far as McKay at least was concerned he came damned close. What they really missed was the sense that the strange, scarred, one-eyed figure was somehow watching over them wherever they were, the knowledge that behind them always stood Crenna, backing them up. He had been a sort of touchstone, a talisman. And now he was gone, lost in the destruction of the vast Heartland complex, which he had blown up around himself to deny the supersecret facility and the vital Blueprint data it contained to the invading FSE expeditionary forces. The Guardians felt in a sense adrift.

Fuck it, McKay told himself. They were grownups; they didn't need big daddy Crenna to hold their hands. But, damn, this one was going to be a bitch.

The proprietor came sauntering back with McKay's

Coke. It was in a green bottle, deeply fluted, of an old-fashioned sort McKay could just barely remember from his own childhood. He suspected it had probably been laid down about the time of the Korean War, but he accepted it readily enough when the old man held it up for his approval, took it when the top was pried off and gulped a deep swallow. It was cool only in comparison to the stifling day around him, and had a moderately peculiar taste to it, but McKay didn't mind. Life after the Holocaust was not for the persnickety.

"That'll be a dime and a half, gentlemen," the old man said. "I sorry it so expensive, but you know how things is. Them salvagers don't work for free, and the reg'lators is always coming around, looking for they taxes."

Sloan came forward, rummaging in the pocket of his trousers for the money. "Regulators? Who are they, anyway?"

The old man set his lips and shook his head. "Now, don't you mind them none. They leave you alone, you boys in that big old armored car of yours, but it don't do a poor man like me no good to be talking about 'em."

Sam started to press, but then McKay caught his eye and gave his head a microscopic shake. Instead Sloan fished out a pair of dimes, dated 1957 and 1963, handed them across to the old man.

Maggie Connoly had thrown a fit when she found out that the representatives of the government of the United States of America were trafficking in gold and silver. She had insisted that the Guardians take with them a sheaf of prototype new dollars that she had got up in some print shop somebody had been convinced to run. Just for shits and grins, the Guardians had tried to pass the things in payment for a couple of rabbits to a roadside trader in western Kentucky. The man had declined after much laughter, pointing out that he could get a handful of leaves anywhere, and *they* wouldn't leave colored ink stains on his ass when he wiped himself.

The Guardians weren't surprised. During their training they had been briefed to expect that in a shattered America only hard currency and barter would likely be acceptable in all except the least affected areas. They had, in fact, found scarcely any areas little enough affected that the survivors would have any part of prewar paper money. So they went about well supplied with coins of silver and gold which were generally identifiable as such: Krugerrands, long-outlawed but recognizable to almost anybody, Mexican gold pesos, ancient silver dollars, and the standards, pre–1965 (and thus mostly silver) quarters and dimes, which as their briefings had predicted formed the basis for most exchange after the war. Gold pieces were just too valuable for most everyday exchanges; dimes and quarters of silver were just right.

Accustomed as he was to dealing in that tender by now, Sam was still slightly startled when the old man reached back into the pocket of his overalls and produced an old green pair of tin snips, with which he cut one of the dimes in two and handed one half back to Sloan. He'd seen it before, of course, but it still brought home to him how foreign his native land had become.

"I don't mean to pry or nothing," the old man said, pulling a handkerchief from his pocket and dabbing at his brow, "but just where are you boys thinking of taking that big armored car, anyhow? You ain't planning to go no deeper into the swamp, are you?"

The Guardians exchanged looks. "Possibly," Sloan said. "Why do you ask?"

The old man held up his hands. "I don't want no trouble. But you boys better know, they ain't too much farther you can take that baby. Roads ain't been kept up in a mighty long time. And the old swamp, she's moving back in, to take what's hers and maybe then some. Once you run out of road, she swallow that car up without leaving even a trace."

"Well, what if we were thinking of heading into the swamp?" McKay asked.

"That's one bad thing to do, you ask me. Bayou's a bad place these days. Strange things come and go, since the war. And I don't mean just snakes and gators, or even the kind of human snakes come through these parts when the cities died. They strange things in there, mighty strange. Lights in the sky at night. Places where if a man go in he don't come out no more."

Billy McKay had one eye practically closed and the other eyebrow hoisted to a good elevation. "What, this old fuck thinks he's Uncle Remus?" he subvocalized. The tiny pickup taped to his larynx transmitted the words over the other Guardians' bone-conduction earphones.

"Don't go jumping to any conclusions that this is just garden-variety superstition," Sloan said back in the same manner. "He may know something, and he looks scared for real."

McKay turned his look on Sloan, but said nothing.

"You know how things are, old timer," Sloan said cheerfully. "The way things are, it's easy for stories to get started."

The oldster shook his head stubbornly. "Believe what you want to, mister. I done heard the stories—and more'n that. I seen the light floating through the sky out over that swamp. Ain't no airplane ever act like that. And I seen the whole sky light up green one Sunday evening just after sundown, saw that light fly away and then afterwards saw two of them reg'lator fellows all burned down into black mummies, like, in what used to be their truck before something blew the gas tank. I ain't just a superstitious blue-gum nigger, mister."

"No, sir, I don't reckon you are. Sorry if I gave offense."

The old man shook his head. "No, I know you don't mean nothing by it. Shoot, I see how you feel the way you do. I never had no truck with this mumbo jumbo stuff neither. But I seen what I seen, mister, and I got to let it go at that."

They all stood around in slightly strained silence, the Guardians sucking their soft drinks, the old man gazing off south, where a sullen band of trees stretched solidly across the horizon. The sky was getting darker, the heavy wind freshening. "Weather coming in," he remarked, sticking his hands in his pockets.

"Hurricane?" Sloan asked. The Effsees still got some coverage from weather satellites, which meant the Guardians also got it, via their helpful gnomes in the Freehold and occupied California. They didn't show any sign of hurricanes threatening this section of coast. On the other hand, this was the season of storms, and the coverage wasn't complete.

"Naw," the old man said. "Don't have the feel of it."

He studied his customers and their unusual vehicle for a moment. "I tell you boys something. You could have took anything you wanted from me, with those big guns of yours in that there turret. But you come along and ask pretty as you please, and even pay afterward. I reckon you must be from the gummint, and got some kind of business what ain't none of mine. But if you head on down a ways, down to where Piegon use to be, then turn off west at the old Kentucky Chicken billboard sign a couple mile on, you come to a place where you can find people. They got a redbone boy down there, name of Andres Daw. You looking for something in the bayou country, he can help you find it; he know this whole coast from Port Arthur to Barataria. Tell him old Whitey sent you; he might help you out."

The Guardians polished off their drinks and handed the bottles back to the old man. "Thanks a lot," Sam Sloan said. "We appreciate the advice."

The old man looked at the sky again. The trees to the south had begun to fuzz out behind an advancing curtain of rain. "Let me give you one more bit, boys. If you out in the swamps and you hear the critters begin to take on, all the animals screaming and the birds crying out like they damned souls or something, you tuck out for the high ground fast. It mean a hurricane coming on, and a hurricane, she's a powerful bad thing in the swamp."

McKay and Sloan exchanged a look. Uh-*huh*.

"Much obliged, sir," Sloan said. They piled back into the armored car, which pulled away with a peevish farting of its big diesel engine. The old man stood by the road and watched them through the gathering gloom until they were out of sight.

Rain beat on the camouflaged poncho Sam Sloan held over his head as if it were a snare drum. He staggered among live oak trees, his boots sinking into the earth at every step. *Helluva thing for a man to go through just to take a leak,* he thought.

Sloan was a camper, a hiker, and a Sierra Club member, who had spent some time in this part of the world before. Publicly he had nothing but scorn for Billy McKay's surly distaste for the considerable natural beauties of the swampland. Privately he had to admit that sometimes Mother Nature could be a godawmighty pain in the ass.

The onset of darkness, hastened by the storm—which came in like a locomotive with no brakes—had forced the Guardians to laager in for the night before proceeding to

Andres Daw's place. Casey Wilson had the eyes and reflexes of a cat, and Mobile One carried all kinds of nifty
night-vision gear, but the rain and the unchecked undergrowth a year of such rains had called up out of the ground
conspired to defeat them. The swamp had reclaimed a lot
of its own, and if the ten-metric-ton V-450 blundered off
the end of a flooded-out road into a deep bog, the odds
were good neither it nor any of the Guardians would come
back up again. They had found an asphalted area back
from the main road, such as it was, with woods on three
sides and a swamp on the other that probably had swal-
lowed up the fast-food store or whatever this had once been
the parking lot for, and settled in to wait for day.

Now Sam was fighting the storm to answer an age-old
call. He had just gotten in behind some discreet willow
trees and startled fumbling for his fly when a bright light
caught him full in the face and a voice growled, "Just what
you think you doing here, boy?"

He stood there for a moment, jacklighted like a deer.
"He got him a *as*-sault rifle, Luther," a younger voice said.

The man holding the huge hand-spot on him loomed
huge behind the light's nova glare. Clearly visible in the
backwash of the beam was a big pump shotgun with a
police-type magazine extension. Blinded and befuddled
and with his fly open as he was, Sloan could tell this was
not a very bright thing to do; the guy was going to have to
make a choice between hanging on to his spotlight and
firing his weapon more than once, if push came to shove.
The man's tone of voice indicated he wasn't very accustomed to push *coming* to shove. Not too surprising, maybe
—it took a lot of nerve or stone craziness to argue with a
leveled twelve-gauge.

"Good evening, gentlemen," Sloan said with his best
conciliatory country twang. "What can I do for you?"

"Explain what you doin' out in these woods with a big

old automatic rifle without the regulators give you permission," the shotgun-and-spotlight boy growled.

"And just who might these regulators be?"

"Us'n," said the younger voice, with an Adam's-apple jiggling titter.

"Well, I'm sorry if I ran afoul of any local ordinances. I was just out here answering the call of nature. If you'll excuse me, I'll just tend to that and get right back inside and not cause any more difficulties—"

"Sure talks smart, don't he, Luther?"

"Shut up, Willie Earl. Mister, what you gone do now is turn right round and march back toward your vehicle peaceable-like, and then we'll drive over to headquarters and ask you a few questions about how you come to be trespassing and carrying illegal type weapons."

" 'Trespassing?' "

"You got a permit signed by the regulators to be out and around here? Well, then, boy, you trespassing. Now, *move*."

Sloan was tempted. He was really tempted. Luther had his Remington pump, and from the outlines of the gangly shadow that was Willie Earl the kid was carrying an FN-FAL assault rifle himself, and they thought they were invincible. One good look at Mobile One and their shit would, as Billy McKay inelegantly but succinctly put it, turn right to water. On the other hand, McKay would give Sloan grief for being an effete college-boy black-shoe Navy man if he needed help busting loose from a pair of peckerwood vigilantes.

"Sorry," he said evenly, "I can't oblige you."

Willie Earl giggled nervously. "Hey, you stupid or what, buster? We got guns, can't you see?"

"Oh yes. And can't you see what'll happen if you shoot a man at point-blank range when he's wearing a chest full of *these?*" Sloan pulled up his poncho to reveal the ripstop vest he wore, its pockets bulging with 40-mm rounds. These two probably didn't know a launcher grenade from a can of Raid, but the fact that the things looked like dumpy bullets gave a pretty solid clue as to their nature.

Willie Earl made a strangled sound around his adenoids and backed away. "He's bluffing, you damn fool," Luther growled. "Them things go off, he's gonna be a sight worse off than we—"

"I tell you boys what," Sam said. He plucked a grenade like an aluminum pomegranate from his belt, held it up, and pulled the pin. "My buddy Billy McKay taught me a little game. It's called 'grenade duel.' And the way you play it is like—"

He released the safety lever and dropped the shiny metal sphere into the mud at his feet. "—this."

"*Holy shit!*" Luther screamed.

The big spotlight fell into the muck, its beam slashing wildly about like a fiery sword. *Just like McKay says, assholes and elbows,* was Sloan's quick impression of his erstwhile captors' vigorous retreat as illuminated by the fallen lantern. Then he thought, *I sure hope McKay's right about how this works,* and went down, rolling himself into a fetus ball with his hands over his head and his back to the grenade to let his Kevlar body armor take the fragments.

It was like being God's own soccer ball for a good penalty kick, and Sloan thought his ears would ring for six weeks. But when McKay came stumbling out with his huge M-60E3 at the ready, and Mobile One fired up like a tyrannosaurus waking up mad, its own huge spotlight flaring forth and its turret swinging around, he was on his feet and almost steady.

"What the fuck happened?" McKay demanded. The rain wet down his short blond stubble of crewcut and made him look even more bullet-headed than usual, which Sloan thoughtfully refrained from pointing out.

Over the 1200-cycle tone in his ears Sloan heard an engine fire up, turned to see headlights veer crazily through the trees and take off up the main road. "Had a little run-in with our friends the regulators." His voice sounded as if it were coming from far away.

"What did they want?"

"Seemed to think they were the only law east of the Pecos. I disabused them of the notion."

"What happened to your poncho? Looks like a lawn-mower ran over your back."

"We played a little game," Sam said. "They lost."

CHAPTER
SEVEN ————————————————————

At the sound of a footfall on the porch of the clap-board cabin, June-Marie spun from the sink. Belatedly she cursed herself for a fool. *I should have run when that boat blew up in the bay this afternoon.*

She had been ready to flee the moment she heard the growl of the patrol boat's engine beating off the bay clear up the little nameless bayou by which her house stood; she had heard that sound before. She had slipped down to the reeds at the verge of the bay to see if the raiders planned to land nearby or only sought shelter from the coming storm. Instead, to her amazement, the intruding craft had blown up within minutes of her arrival with a tremendous orange flash.

She guessed that something had made its gas tanks ex-plode—the missile that actually killed it had burned its propellant fuel out within seconds of launch, and had coasted most of the way to its target, steering by means of its vanes, so that from shore several kilometers away June-Marie never saw it strike its fleeing target. From the size of the blast, she expected no survivors. She had not been unhappy. A raiding party from that very boat had sacked her house once. Though she had few friends remaining on this coast, savaged by weather and disease, she had lost some to raiders from the sea in the awful year since the war.

There had been a time when she would have taken her little boat and rowed out to see if she could locate and help survivors, no matter who they'd been. No more. She had learned hard lessons in the last year.

And now she had forgotten one. At the first sign of trouble she should have slipped from her cabin, even if she had done no more than pull back into the cover of the trees and Spanish moss, watched and waited until she was sure there was no threat. The house perched on stilts at water's edge was too obvious, too inviting.

But she hated to leave her home, the little house where her parents had lived, her brother and sisters, before they had gone their separate ways to seek what fortunes they could find in the world beyond the bayous. She had come back here, even though there was a place for her where the ravages of the war were scarcely felt. She belonged here, and she hated to leave.

But now her stubbornness—or her lethargy, perhaps—had cost her. With sick certainty she knew the storm's growing noise must have covered the sound of a second ship entering the bay. She wheeled from the kitchen into the front room. Someone was trying the latch on the front door, and on the thin chintz curtain she could see the shadows of people moving around on the porch, cast by the last dying daylight.

"Damn," she said softly. Maybe the back way . . . a few steps from her back door, and only the keenest of bayou hunters would have any chance at all of tracking her through the dark woods and twisting channels she and her brother had run free as children. She spun.

A bearded face grinned through the screen of the back door at her. She gasped, wheeled for the drainboard where a butcher knife lay. The door burst open and then the man was in the kitchen, pot-bellied and bandy-legged, in a green and brown camouflage smock and a battered hat of the same pattern. He smelled of sweat and diesel oil. Across his belly he held a stubby rifle with a folded stock and a banana-shaped magazine that she recognized from TV newscasts as being Russian.

She snatched up the knife and menaced him, crouching low, circling to her right, ready to spring past him out the open door if he brought the weapon up. Too late she heard a warped board creak behind her, started to pivot right, checked, lunged full-out for the door.

A strong hand caught her left wrist. She rolled her wrist in toward her and out again, gashing her attacker's own wrist with the knife. She heard a curse in what she thought was Spanish, then the first man had her in a bear hug from behind, lifting her not inconsiderable weight off the floor, grunting in exertion and pain as she hammered her bare heels into his shins. Her long dark hair whipped her face as she tried to drive her head back to smash his nose, cause him to ease his grip for the fraction of a second that was all she needed for escape.

Two men had come in through the front door as she menaced the first. One picked up a rickety wooden chair from the kitchen table and batted the knife out of her hand with it. He was laughing. The other, a taller man with a scar across his heavy face, left off clutching his blood-spurting wrist to backhand her massively across the face. Her head snapped around. He hit her a return stroke with his open palm, and then again backhand, back, forth. The man who had hold of her spat angry syllables. The man with the chair, more slender and younger than the others, grabbed the big man's arm before he could strike again. He spoke low and urgently to the man.

She eyed him through tangles of her long hair, fighting the silly urge to gratitude that welled up within her. She wasn't a child. She had no illusions that he had stopped his compatriot from beating her unconscious or even to death for humanitarian motives.

She was right. While she was still hanging there groggy in the pot-bellied man's arms the others stripped off her jeans, the man she'd slashed using a knife from his own belt to cut off the buttons at the fly, looking at her with a shine to his eye that made her blood cold. They tore open her flannel shirt. Then they took turns raping her on the kitchen floor, while the storm wind hammered on the eaves and darkness swelled to fill the little house.

When his turn came the scar-faced man abraded her cheek with his beard and gobbled endearments in broken English. She kept her face averted and willed her mind to nothingness.

When they had finished they left the big-bellied man to watch over her while they searched the house. She huddled against the wall with the slashed remnants of her shirt clutched about her and fought not to moan. Eventually they came back holding the only firearm in the house, an ancient single-barreled break-open shotgun, with a handful of twenty-gauge shells in a cheesecloth bag. Gloating at her, scar-face broke it open and then, holding it by the barrel, smashed its butt repeatedly against the doorjamb, until the receiver was bent way out of true and would no longer close on a shell. Then he tossed the ruined gun in the living room.

She watched the little pantomime with steady eyes. When it was over, she stood up, started back for the bedroom. The bearded man caught her arm. "I have to get clothes," she said, her own voice rusty in her ears.

They debated this for a couple of minutes. She strained, trying to fit their speech into a year's high school Spanish, but the rapid colloquial conversation and Caribbean accent defeated her. In any event, the positions seemed clear enough; the younger, slimmer one thought she should be allowed to do as she asked, Scarface, now with a field dressing on his hand, seemed to feel it would be a turn-on to leave her just the way she was, with the shredded tail of her shirt hanging down almost to the cigarette burn he'd put on her rump. At last the pot-bellied man with the beard spoke. He seemed the closest thing to a leader of this trio, and the scarred man's heavy face darkened.

"You go dress," the young one said then in heavily accented English. "Then come cook dinner. Don' try tricks, we don' hurt you."

She throttled the impulse to laugh hysterically. Instead she started back for her room thinking, *it can't be this easy.* It wasn't.

"Wait. Luis go with," the youngster said. Pot-belly came ambling after her with his rifle tucked under his arm, looking for all the world like an English baron out hunting on his estate in some TV movie.

He followed her through the living room, past the silent glass box of the television, past the ancient brass clock on its shelf beside an old flatiron and a couple of books, its ticking somehow loud even against the pervasive roar of the storm. She felt an undercurrent of fear as to what the man might do when they were alone. But when he'd made use of her, he'd seemed almost detached, somehow, and now he stood by not even seeming to watch her as she dressed quickly in another pair of jeans and a similar shirt to the one she'd been wearing.

She didn't even toy with the notion of trying anything

cinematic, such as grabbing the weapon from him, or simply ripping open the screened window and diving out into the rain. The man had too familiar a way with his evil-looking rifle, and his posture was that of relaxed readiness, not overconfidence. And the stakes would be high, she guessed, if she tried anything and failed; now that their immediate animal lusts were sated for the moment, they might have fewer scruples about killing her out of hand.

She padded back into the kitchen to find the other two soldiers sitting at the table by the light of a single kerosene lamp. The big-bellied man pulled in a chair from the front room, set it with its back against the back door, which was flapping in the wind with its latch broken, sat down with his weapon cradled across his knees.

"You fix us dinner now, babee," Scarface said. "Fix us something good."

The first thing she did was open the cupboard next to the wood-burning stove and get out two quarts of home-made blackberry wine in Paul Masson bottles and set them on the table. The soldiers raised appreciative eyebrows. "Eee, she know how to treat us right," the scarred man said. His younger comrade, eyes downcast, murmured thanks. He seemed to be enjoying second thoughts about this whole thing.

She let them work on the bottles while she busied herself boiling up a pot of greens and preparing a fresh-caught catfish for dinner. When she had to fill a pail with cooking water—fuel to run the pump for the tap in the sink was a luxury she couldn't afford—her ever-present escort followed her out and stood by while she filled it from a hand pump in the yard, then followed her back in like an obedient bulldog.

As the levels in the bottles dropped, the men began to relax. The bearded man had a dispute with the scarred one for possession of one of the half-empty bottles; she let it go on for a moment, then opened the refrigerator, which stood silently to one side—even with no power to run it, its insulation still made it useful for cool storage. She produced two more bottles, one more homemade wine in a Gallo bottle, the other a real treasure, an unopened bottle of Beefeater's gin, which she never touched but had brought back from New Orleans against a visit her brother never made. She set these on the table, and Scarface abruptly allowed Luis to return to his chair with the full wine bottle in his possession.

Halfway through the meal Scarface stopped, picked up the gin bottle, eyed it suspiciously. "You try to make us drunk?" he demanded.

She didn't look up from stirring salvaged sugar into a pot of water heating on the fire. "I can make tea."

With a decisive motion Scarface screwed the cap back on the Beefeater's. "We save for later. Wine, she don't make us drunk."

"You don't want tea?"

He laughed.

Outside the storm moaned like a cat in heat. Rain fell in furious waves. The kitchen filled up with steamy, caramelly aroma as the pot came to a boil once more. She poured in half a bottle of molasses—made since the war, not salvage—stirred it into the thick steaming mess with a long-handled wooden spoon.

"What you make there?" Scarface demanded as she cleaned the dishes away from the table.

"Dessert."

She collected the heavy earthenware plates from the man by the door, plunked them down beside the sink and began to scrub them in the pail with homemade soap. Luis began to stir by the door, loosening his web belt with his thumb and shifting his legs. After a moment he said something in Spanish to his comrades, rose, pulled the chair away from the front door and went out into the storm. "Don' get lost," Scarface called after him.

She came over to the table, bent down to adjust the lamp. Her blue and black checked shirt, which had been buttoned to the top button, had somehow come undone to her sternum. The youngest of the trio had surreptitiously appropriated the gin bottle and was preoccupied by that, but Scarface helped himself to a lingering glance at her full breasts swaying gently in shadow as she bent down. Thoughtfully, he rubbed his chin.

She returned to the stove, swaying her hips ever so slightly as she walked. *Dear God, don't let me overplay my hand*. She stood at the stove, agitating the bubbling mixture with the spoon. In a moment she heard the creak and scrape of a chair being drawn back, the clump of jungle boots on bare pine flooring, felt hot humid breath on the back of her neck as a heavy hand scooped up her long hair. "Ah, *querida*—" Scarface began, bending to nuzzle her neck.

She turned around and threw the contents of the pot full in his face.

He shrieked like a damned soul as the boiling mass covered him and clung, burning like napalm.

He turned, ran full tilt into the silent refrigerator, rebounded, clawing at the bubbling, seething mass of boiling sugar. The stink of burning hair slashed across the air of the room.

The youthful soldier was just coming up out of his chair when his howling comrade blundered into the table and knocked it over on his legs. He went down to one knee, blinking in befuddlement, his feet tangled with his chair. June-Marie grabbed bearded Luis's empty wine bottle from beside the door. The boy made a feeble gesture to defend himself as she smashed it down on his forehead. He went down with blood splashing down his face. She scooped up his AKMS assault rifle by the sling and dodged around the edge of the doorway into the front room.

She turned, crouched, poked the muzzle of the rifle back into the kitchen. Scarface was rolling mindlessly back and forth between the icebox and the upset table, kicking spastically, his palms welded to the mass of molten sugar and flesh that had been his face. He raised a rising-falling howl like an air-raid siren.

The stubby rifle weighed heavy and alien in June-Marie's hands. She pointed it at the foot of the back screen. She knew that the kick of the weapon on automatic fire would bring its barrel up. That was all she knew. She prayed to the Virgin for the first time in years, prayed the safety wasn't on, prayed the crafty Luis would not think to play this professionally cool. If he did, she had no chance.

He didn't. He came scrabbling up the rain-slick plank steps holding his AK by the receiver, his fly gaping comically open. There were three of them, after all, and their victim was only a woman—and the wine, while it hadn't made him drunk, had dulled his wits and instincts just a hair. He threw open the door and lunged into the kitchen.

June-Marie fired. She was well aware that there was an art to shooting the thing, of which she had not the first clue. She just gripped the forestock and pistol grip as tightly as possible, snugged the metal stock to her shoulder as though she were firing a shotgun, and held down the trigger. Yellow-orange muzzle flashes lit the room more brightly than the lantern, now dying on its side in the corner. Huge splinters of pine flew everywhere. The noise was mind-shattering.

The recoil was no worse than the shotguns Marie had fired thousands of times. She couldn't hold the muzzle down, though, didn't try, just battled to hold the weapon on-line on the doorway as it roared and flamed. She saw the soldier's face, screaming mouth ringed by heavy beard, eerily underlit by the muzzle flashes. He did a queer little jig amid a shower of wood chips and broken crockery, then fell backward out the door as the bullet stream buzzsawed into the lintel.

June-Marie released her death grip on the trigger. Silence struck her like a mallet blow. Through the ringing in her ears she heard a brief chiming tinkle as the last few spent cases jittered on the floorboards. The palms of both hands tingled, and to calm her spinning mind she made herself draw a deep breath before poking her head and the rifle out the door.

The pot-bellied soldier's gun lay just inside the door. She stalked carefully forward, nonetheless slipped once and stifled a yelp as her bare foot trod on a hot cartridge. She righted herself, peered cautiously out the door, assault rifle ready.

Luis lay sprawled head down at the foot of the steps. His camouflage tunic and trousers were stained by big dark blotches that ran in the rain. Through the din of the storm it seemed that she could hear him breathing, a thin, gurgling, whining sound. He did not seem much of a threat.

She went back inside. She had a sudden impulse to throw the rifle away from her, realized that might make it go off, bent down and placed it on the floorboards with exaggerated care. The burned man was huddled against the wall making gobbling sounds. The youngest soldier lay motionless beside the table. She knelt, pulled off his belt, lashed his wrists tightly at the small of his back. She went briefly through his kit, pulled out several of what she took to be protein bars, appropriated his canteen.

She went into the back room, emerged in moments with a long Cordura case and a dark green knapsack—bayou folk didn't go in much for the bright orange and red sacks hikers wore hoping hunters wouldn't take them for deer; when they were out and about they generally preferred not to be seen at all. She had on a pair of old running shoes, also dark green. She packed some dried meat and fruit from the cold box, took the bound man's sheath knife and fastened it to her own belt. Then she ran down the steps, jumped the still-breathing body of the bearded soldier, and disappeared into the rain and trees.

CHAPTER
EIGHT ──────────────

"Gentlemen, I am sorry. I know nothing of any secret facility in the vicinity. I am sure none of my people do, either." John Tourond, mayor of what the hurricanes had left of the little town of Cocodrie, near the west end of Terrebonne Bay, was a man of middle years and middle size, with thinning brown hair and something of a beard, streaked with gray at the edges of his chin, and slightly popped, heavily lidded eyes. "I assure you, we will do everything we can to cooperate."

Colonel Correy eyed him without favor from his seat behind his desk in the cabin he'd taken for his office on the *General Marshall*'s upper deck. The porthole was open, but the air drifting in from the white-hot morning outside was sluggish, stifling. Yesterday's storm hadn't cooled things down any.

"They damned well better, Mr. Mayor," he rapped.

Mancuso shifted his weight from foot to foot. Correy held up a square callused hand and shook his head. "I apologize, Mr. Mayor. I spoke out of turn. But you have to realize what's at stake here. The future of America, and quite possibly the whole of the free world."

"I'm sure that His Honor Mr. Tourond understands the import of the situation—" Captain Mancuso began.

"Don't start, Francis."

"Perhaps if the colonel could tell me a little more specifically what he is looking for?"

Correy eyed Tourond for a moment, chewing on his underlip. He dropped his open palm heavily to the metal surface of the desk. PO Myers shot him a warning look. He ignored it. "I suppose it can't hurt to give you some idea. What we are looking for is some kind of government facility."

The mayor shrugged. "Houma Air Force Base is ten, twenty miles up Bayou Terrebonne. It's abandoned, of course."

Myers raised a pale eyebrow. "'Of course'?"

Another shrug. "Plague. Cleaned them right out. Cleaned most of this coast out. Some of us here in these smaller towns stuck it out, others ran for it. Don't know if it did them any good. The older folks say the Four Horsemen are loose on the world, that it does no good to run and hide. I don't know but that they might be right."

"Then why did you stay, if you don't mind my asking, Mr. Mayor?" Correy asked.

"This is my home, Colonel. As soon die here as anywhere."

Myers sat on a corner of the desk, drawing an irritated look from the colonel, crossed his lanky legs, and folded his hands across one knee. "Folks are religious hereabouts? Do they follow Reverend Smith's broadcasts, out of Oklahoma?"

"Not hardly. People are good Catholics in these parts."

Myers nodded, as if this confirmed something he'd known all along. "This facility is secret—" Mancuso began.

"Then you'd hardly expect me or my people to know about it, then, would you?"

Mancuso smiled thinly, made an easy gesture, conceding the point. "But I wonder if an installation of any size could really be kept secret from people who know the country."

Tourond set his jaw, nodded. "You got a point there, son."

"What Captain Mancuso is driving at, Mr. Mayor," Myers said, "is that perhaps some of your townsfolk do know something of this installation, without your being aware—"

"Begging your pardon, sir, but what I was driving at was that the people that built this base might have realized they couldn't keep it a total secret. They might have let out that it was meant for something else," said Mancuso.

Tourond raised a bushy eyebrow. "The people who built it? I thought you said the government built it."

Myers was now looking vexed at Mancuso. "Well, different parts of the government do different things, Your Honor."

The mayor looked thoughtful. "Well, we had some oil rigs hereabouts, till they got shut down. Aside from the military boys, most of the government stuff around here was wildlife refuges, things like that. You wouldn't be looking for a wetlands wildlife research center, would you?"

"Thank you, Mr. Mayor, but I'm afraid that's hardly the sort of thing we're looking for," Myers said.

"Well, have you heard any rumors about any kind of, ah, unusual activities in this vicinity?" asked Mancuso, grasping rather obviously for straws.

A shadow seemed to flicker across Tourond's broad face. "No—nothing."

Abruptly, Correy stood. "Well, Mr. Mayor, I don't see any reason to take any more of your time. We do appreciate any help you or your townspeople can give us." He gave Tourond's hand a quick shake.

Tourond started out. "Mr. Mayor—" Myers said. Tourond stopped. "You are a loyal American, aren't you?"

Frowning, the mayor said, "Yes, sir. I am a loyal *American*."

"And you realize that we are representatives of the rightful government of the United States of America?"

Gray eyes flicked to the blue-and-white FSE patches sewn above the American flags on the officers' upper sleeves. "Yes, sir. We've always been patriotic folk hereabouts." He vanished out into the passageway.

Myers studied the deck over their heads. "I don't like his attitude."

"You got some argument with patriotism?" Correy almost barked.

Myers shrugged lightly. "I suppose not."

Correy turned back to the papers on his desk. "We'd better start sending patrols up these damned bayous. We'll use power boats for the most part. Requisition some from the locals if we don't have enough."

"What about the hovercraft, sir?" Mancuso asked.

"They're too damned temperamental. I don't want to run up too many hours on their clocks unnecessarily. Besides, they represent what heavy firepower we've got—unless one of you gentlemen can think of a way to make our tanks float?"

Neither man said anything. "Then I'll let you two get back to your duties, gentlemen."

• • •

Myers paced Mancuso down the passageway. "Our colonel is a very dedicated soldier, Captain," the gangly political officer remarked.

Mancuso kept his eyes front. "Yes, sir. He is that."

"But I'm afraid he has none too firm a grasp of the political realities. It's a common failing among even the better line officers." His pale eyes looked sidelong at the captain. "I'd appreciate it if you'd do me a little favor, Captain."

Mancuso started to frown, checked himself. "What might that be, sir?"

"I'd be really grateful if our patrols could provide me with a few of the locals to talk to. Townsfolk, of course, but better yet people from out among the bayous. They'll have a better idea of what might be going on back in the swamps."

Mancuso stopped at the foot of a ladder. "Are you asking me to go behind Colonel Correy's back, sir?"

"I wouldn't ask anything dishonorable of you, Captain. And you might remember that under the enlightened administration of the FSE the political infrastructure supersedes the military chain of command. So it's perfectly all right for you to follow my instructions. As for Colonel Correy—"

Myers looked off at nothing in particular. "He's a splendid officer, really splendid. But he has enough responsibilities without having to concern himself with, shall we say, the intelligence end of things."

Mancuso looked at the highly shined tips of his shoes. "Yes, sir," he said, quietly.

Myers patted him on the shoulder. "We got excellent reports about you when you were with Staff at Antwerp. You've got quite a career ahead of you." And with that he was gone, up into the milky daylight.

• • •

"End of the road, gentlemen," said Andres Daw as Casey braked Mobile One to a halt.

They had penetrated five or six klicks past the deserted Houma Air Force Base. Now the blacktop road suddenly dipped out of sight beneath an expanse of murky water that stretched out before them for what looked like a kilometer before fetching up against a treelined shore. Hunkered down behind Sam Sloan to peer through the Electronic Systems Officer's vision block, McKay glanced sourly at the guide.

"Our maps say this road goes on a ways."

Daw gestured with a hand like a cluster of boiled hot dogs. "As you can see, they're a bit outdated. That little war of yours brought storms like this coast has never seen, and consequently a good deal of State Highway 57 now runs along the bottom of Boudreaux Lake. Town of Boudreaux's down there, too."

"It wasn't *our* war," said Casey Wilson, lifting his yellow Zeiss shooting glasses to wipe sweat from the bridge of his nose. The normally mellow Southern California–born pilot sounded almost testy. Andres Daw was exactly the sort to rub even the most easygoing Guardian the wrong way.

"But with the EPA shutting down the oil rigs, FDA regulations closing down the sugar plantations, and the restrictions on fishing this stretch of coast, there wasn't much of anybody left to speak of in Boudreaux, anyway. Government didn't care enough to leave them any way to feed themselves, so I don't guess it ought to bother you much about their being under water."

McKay eyed him without great joy. "Daw, you are a real pleasure."

The guide did not respond. McKay had the distinct feeling he didn't care whether he made the Guardians uncom-

fortable or not. God knew he wasn't much to look at. He
was big, maybe six-two, with a head like a cut-down keg,
massive features that managed to be at once craggy and
bloated, a broad nose, eyes like slits, curly black hair
dusted with gray fringing a great shining lump of skull. His
shoulders and chest were large, and a belly of truly heroic
proportions hung over his khaki shorts, barely contained by
a grimy white T-shirt, over which he wore what looked as
if it might at one point have been the vest to a three-piece
suit, black with fine blue pinstripes. His legs looked incon-
gruously thin, sinewy almost, with great knobby knees and
vast splayed feet shod in Ho Chi Minh slippers made out of
old chunks of tire. A short-barreled .38-caliber revolver
snuggled in a cracked and grimy holster on his right hip.
McKay wondered if maybe, just maybe, their good buddy
Whitey had steered them wrong.

Still, as of this moment Andres Daw comprised the sum
total of their assets in this part of the world. As far as this
mission was concerned, the Guardians definitely belonged
to that class of people who can't be choosers.

"So, ah, where are the folks you were saying you knew,
Mr. Daw?" asked Sam Sloan, indefatigably polite.

An elephantine shrug. "You said you had a boat. You
got a boat?"

"Yeah, we got a boat," McKay said. He and Sloan
deassed the car and went around to break open a conformal
carrying case—which meant a high-tech crate—strapped
to the side of the rear deck aft of the one-man turret. As
they had the day before, the Guardians had forsaken their
usual coveralls for bare chests and cammie trousers. They
had also left off the flexible Kevlar armor they usually
wore under their fatigues; the stuff was a whiz for keeping
out shell fragments and low-velocity rounds, but it was
even better at producing acute discomfort in the humid sort

of heat so abundant hereabouts.

Daw stood by whistling some jazz tune as the two inflated a dark green six-man rubber boat and affixed the low-noise miniature outboard. It figured Daw would like jazz. McKay hated jazz. It never made sense to him, and that irritated him.

From the way Daw was rumpling up his forehead and nose, McKay gathered he didn't think much of the boat. "You boys just couldn't have brought a decent pirogue along with you, could you?"

"These babies are the latest thing, buster," McKay said.

"Like six-hundred-dollar toilet seats?"

McKay scowled. He'd spent too much time in the field to put much faith in government procuring techniques himself. On the other hand, most of the goodies provided to the Guardians worked pretty much as advertised—the late Major Crenna had seen to that—but he was going to look like pretty much of a jerk if he stood here flatfooted and tried to explain all of that.

Daw got saddled up without further complaint and went putting off east along the verge of the expanded lake, edging past the tops of drowned trees. The little motor was almost silent; by the time it had gone twenty meters McKay's sharp ears couldn't pick it up at all. He was halfway tempted to shout out after Daw to point out the fact.

Tom and Casey emerged from the vehicle and the Guardians flaked out around it, keeping their personal long arms handy and never straying far from the cooling car. McKay trudged a few meters off the causeway and sat on reasonably solid ground at the foot of a willow, watching the sunlight dance along the water out through branches that hung like a punk hairdo. Sloan started walking out the kinks in his legs again, while Casey stood at the verge of the water skipping stones. Rogers, the original iron man, apparently had no need for any R&R; he stayed up in the opened turret cleaning the actions of the two big guns.

Casey watched a particularly fine shot, scooting across the water and touching down ever so lightly at intervals like a whippoorwill skimming waterbugs at sunset. "Think we can trust him?" he asked when it finally went down for the last time.

McKay shrugged, digging at a patch of moss-encrusted dirt with a twig, making life difficult for a bunch of black ants marching back and forth in orderly lines.

"I'm not sure," Sloan said. The heavy heat had overcome his urge to exercise, and he was also seeking shelter under the arching branches of the willow. "He was a drug dealer, after all."

"I thought you were into all that civil liberties shit, wouldn't let a little detail like that bother you," McKay jeered.

Sloan frowned; the barb went home. "I do. But I guess I just don't approve of that sort of thing." He shook his head. "Still, I can almost sympathize. People in coastal areas tend mighty strongly to view smuggling as a legitimate occupation. Drugs were surely the most profitable thing to smuggle. And this *was* a depressed area, just as Mr. Daw pointed out."

"There you go, makin' excuses. You should have been an ACLU lawyer."

McKay poked the twig into the earth a little too hard and it snapped off clean. He was giving Sloan shit for the sake of pure art. Although he'd been a real hardass with people who got fucked-up on duty—no matter if it was drugs or booze, it risked everybody's neck, and he wasn't having any of it—he cared jack what people did on their own time. He sure wasn't going to preach morality.

On the other hand, he was not under the impression that

every drug dealer was St. Francis of Assisi. And Andres Daw wasn't precisely the sort to inspire confidence. Following the old man at the former gas station's instructions, they had located him that morning in a swaybacked shack on Lake Verret, in what had been Assumption Parish, where he lived with his vast wife and a beautiful seven-year-old daughter who didn't look as if she could possibly be related to either parent. He had treated them warily from the outset, only admitting his own identity on learning that Whitey had sent the Guardians to him.

He was not impressed when they told him they were on a special secret mission from the government. In fact, his reply had been to tell them point blank that he had run drugs before the war, and were they sure they wanted to bother with scum like him?

They weren't, really, but then again they didn't have much choice. But Daw had seemed even less eager for the deal than they were, and not even promise of payment in gold whipped up his enthusiasm.

"I'll tell you what," he finally said, sitting in the shade on his porch, "I'll guide you into the bayou country and set you up with people who can help you find what you're looking for—*if,* when you find it, or even give up looking —you come back and clean out those damned regulators with that armored car of yours."

"Just what are these regulators, anyway?" Sam had asked, last night's encounter vivid in his memory.

"Heavily armed white trash," Daw explained. "Range from your normal scum to real Klan types—not that the Klan's ever amounted to much in Louisiana, at least since the twenties, and that was only up in Shreveport, never here in the bayous. But times have changed. War seems to have created an environment favorable to a certain kind of parasite."

"Road gypsies with red necks," McKay said.

Daw nodded. "Say they're bringing law and order to this part of Louisiana. Funny how hard it is to tell from a reign of terror."

The Guardians were under no circumstances supposed to go poking into local affairs unnecessarily. But this was important to *the mission*, and anyway these regulators were just the sorts whose asses the Guardians would not mind having a good excuse to kick. They had agreed.

Somewhere a frog hopped into the water with a muffled splash. McKay started, then settled back down, neck burning under Sloan's superior smirk. Hell, he was a city boy, and he'd pulled his service time in decent deserts in the Mediterranean. He'd gone through intensive swamp training with the rest of them when they were learning how to be Guardians, but he was damned if he was comfortable here.

An hour later the inflatable boat came gliding up with Daw at the tiller. With him was a small man in a battered Panama hat, with a huge nose and an even huger black mustache that made him look like a large rat.

"This is Mr. Gariepy," Daw said as the little man nimbly leaped ashore. "He can help us find who we are looking for. And he's got a decent damned boat we can use."

"What about the car?" McKay asked.

"There's a clearing not far away where the ground is solid and it'll be out of sight," Daw said. "I imagine you gents have things you can do to keep somebody from hot-wiring it?"

"You got that right," Billy McKay said.

"They say they don't know nothing about no secret facility, Sarge," the bucktoothed private with a strand of tow-colored hair hanging in his eyes said.

Standing on the end of a little jetty that looked as if it had been laid down when Abe Lincoln was a pup, Staff Sergeant Horatio Gates of the FSE raised his coal-scuttle helmet off his short Afro and wiped his forehead with the back of his hand. "Well now, ain't that a surprise, Luttrell. There's supposed to be a top-secret government hideout somewhere in these swamps, and the people you run into along the bayou don't all know where it is. Imagine that."

Luttrell looked around. "Better not let the SPs hear you talking like that, Sarge." *SPs* meant Special Police, which was what the FSE political watchdogs were being called these days.

Gates spat into coffee-colored water. "Shit." He shook his head. "Hell, the colonel tells us to do it this way, we do it this way. I got to admit I ain't got a better idea."

He gazed across the stream. It was tiny, not ten meters across, with tall trees crowding in on both sides of it, their branches hanging low, draped with Spanish moss like strands of camouflage netting. The surface of the water was a bright lime green; it was covered solid with millions and millions of these little tiny plants.

This was not the kind of country the thirty-eight-year-old sergeant would have chosen to conduct operations in. He was a city boy from East St. Louis, and like all foot-sloggers throughout history he hated mud and wet more than anything.

At least they were able to ride around in boats for the most part. He glanced down at the little motor launch bobbing at his feet with an E-1 sitting in the stern trying not to go to sleep.

"Wish we had one of them blowers," he remarked. "At least a man can have a roof over his head in one of them, keep the sun off."

The buck private in the launch grinned gap-toothed up

at him. "You ought to see if you can get us one of them airboats, Sarge. It would be a lot more fun to drive than this old thing."

"Be busting your neck, we let you loose in one of those, Winfield."

A humongous white bird came flap-flapping down the bayou, ungainly and beautiful as hell, screeching *cuk-cuk, cuk-cuk* as it passed. "Well, hell," the sergeant said, "at least there's pretty stuff to see. Wish I could come here as a tourist."

"Shoot, Sergeant, it ain't nothing but an old swamp," Winfield said.

"You got no feel for the beauties of nature."

A couple more troopies came down from the little house on its stilts, their M-16s slung, their boots thumping hollowly on the jetty. "All right, everybody," Gates said to the rest of the squad, sitting around by the edge of the sluggish water, "let's saddle up and go."

"Uh, Sarge," Luttrell said hesitantly. "The people *did* say something . . ."

Gates looked at him. "Well?"

"They said they just heard a rumor, about a bunch of armed men landing on the coast not too far away from here."

Gates put his hands on his hips. "Well, now, Luttrell, congratulations. You done found out about us. Maybe we ought to transfer you to Intelligence."

"No, Sarge, you don't understand. These people knew about us too. It's some other group they was talking about."

"News travels mighty quick up these bayous," said Hawthorn, a black private from Shreveport, in the northwestern part of the state.

Gates scratched at the corner of his neat mustache.

"Damn. This is gonna complicate things. Sanchez, get on the horn to battalion. I got a feeling they're going to want to know about this."

CHAPTER
NINE ───────────────────

The fat little white dog with one lopped ear wagged
its tail and yapped at the closed flap of the tent. "Come in,
Lieutenant," Asusta called from the card table he was using
as a desk.

"How did you know it was me?" his elegant executive
officer asked, stooping to enter. The dog bounced around
his immaculate shoes.

"Neruda told me." Asusta indicated a camp stool.
"Have a seat. The ground cloth keeps the furniture from
sinking into the earth too rapidly."

Cardenas hiked up his knife-creased trousers and sat.
"You could find more suitable quarters in one of the abandoned habitations along the shore, Captain."

"The truly abandoned ones are filled with mud and ver-
min. The ones whose owners fled when we turned up

aren't necessarily in much better shape. And some of their owners are still hanging around, if the sniping incidents I've been getting reports on are any indication. Neruda, come here."

He scooped the dog up and rubbed its sleek round head, frowning. The worst incident had taken place the very evening they had arrived, when a scouting party of three of Maestre's marines met with disaster at an innocent-seeming shack up one of the innumerable streams feeding into the bay. One man had died, of multiple gunshot wounds, on the launch back to the ship; another had been savagely burned on the face, shoulders, and hands; the third had been concussed from a blow on the head. Asusta and the sergeant had browbeaten the truth out of the one who had gotten hit on the head: a bit of rape gone awry.

Asusta had spoken sharply to Maestre about the lack of discipline among his men. The burned man had had his throat slit and been rolled overboard. He was blinded, his hands crippled, almost certain to develop terrible infections in this hothouse; for his part, Commander Asusta was disinclined to waste the precious supply of pain killers, antibiotics, and other medication on a hopeless case. The youthful survivor of the trio was in the brig. There would be no charges—some things you had to overlook in what was, after all, wartime—but it would do the fool good to cool his heels for a while.

"I don't see why the captain felt it necessary to leave his comfortable quarters on the ship to camp out in this swamp," Cardenas said in the formal way he had when skirting his commander's temper.

"Because I had an urge to feel solid ground beneath my feet. Unfortunately, this was the best we could do."

Cardenas was from the relatively dry uplands of the eastern mountains; he had taken to life asea with a con-

vert's fervor. Commander Asusta—who was always referred to as "Captain," following an ancient tradition of
nautical courtesy—on the other hand, was from a fishing
village on the south coast, had grown up with boats and
chosen the Navy as an escape from the grinding daily labor
of plying the nets. He was a natural-born sailor who loved
and hated the sea and had secret fantasies of being an al-
pinist. So it went.

"How are the repairs coming, comrade?" he asked.

The exec shrugged. "Engineering thinks they can get the
starboard booster to run without shaking itself to pieces.
But we're not going to get even half the rated boost power
to the starboard shaft until we get her to some sort of decent shipyard."

"And where might we find that, my friend? We can
hardly go home. The damned Trotskyite revisionists
who've taken over would sink us on sight. Not that the
yanqui bombers left much of the Cienfuegos Naval Station."

"Central America—"

"You know as well as I, Comrade Lieutenant, that the
Brazilian Navy is getting increasingly aggressive. They
take a dim view of competition in waters their expansionist
tendencies lead them to regard as theirs. *They* didn't suffer
thermonuclear bombardment, after all. And their vessels
are armed with license-built Exocet IIs, longer-ranged than
the imitations the Russians sold us."

Asusta goaded Neruda off his lap, rose, walked to the
flap and held it open, gazing out at his ship, low and sleek
and lethal in close-hanging haze. *She is beautiful, the
bitch.* "I think our destiny lies here, my friend," he said
without turning.

"Captain?"

Asusta half-turned. "The richest nation on earth," he

said, gesturing with his hand, "grown fat with wealth wrung from oppressed peoples of half the earth. Just lying there, waiting to be claimed. By us, if we have the courage to confront our world-historical mission."

The lieutenant sat looking at him with upraised eyebrows. This foray had started as a simple raiding—"expropriating"—expedition to the southern coast of North America. Now it seemed to have taken on an entirely new dimension in the commander's mind.

"I recall the captain's making a joke along those lines when we entered the bay," Cardenas said. "May I remind the comrade captain, there are barely two hundred of us."

"Ah, but we have *Cienfuegos*."

Cardenas cocked a skeptical brow. "How can you hope to conquer a continent with a single frigate?"

Asusta laughed. "Probably I can't. But think of the great imperialist Cortez, who conquered the powerful Aztec empire with a handful of men."

"With the help of a few tens of thousands of Indian allies," Cardenas said sourly.

"Of course, of course. But he didn't bring them from Cuba, did he? The forces of history used Cortez to their own ends." He walked back to the paper-littered table. "Need I remind you that the triumph of world revolution is inevitable, the setback suffered by our former Soviet allies notwithstanding?"

"Of course not." Cardenas looked scandalized.

Asusta nodded. "Then is it so hard to believe that history might thrust into our hands the means of setting revolution once more in motion along the path to victory?"

The lieutenant looked at his immaculately manicured nails. "I—I really cannot say, Captain."

Asusta laughed. "Well, it's fun to believe, at any rate. We have *Cienfuegos*, and she spells power. Why not use her as best we can?"

The house stood proud and white, two stories tall, with a steeply pitched roof and a wide veranda. It all looked very grand and antebellum, especially with the darkness to cover up the peeling whitewash and missing roof tiles and the other signs of decay. It was located between the northern portion of Lake Mechant and Bayou du Large, virtually midway between Atchafalaya Bay and Terrebonne Bay, on a couple of acres of solid ground, mostly reclaimed from the swamp decades past and not yet repossessed, as so much more recently developed land had been. Torchlight washing across its facade like gusts of rain particularly flattered the old house, as candlelight flatters an aging woman.

Sam Sloan and Billy McKay stood off by a lone tupelo gum tree to one side of the circle of torches. A dozen men clustered around a picnic table loaded down with platters of fish, pots of gumbo, and innumerable bottles of dubious provenance. Sam gestured at the flamelight dancing on the front of the house. "Somehow this reminds me of the burning of Atlanta in *Gone with the Wind*."

McKay took the cigarette out of his mouth. "No shit?" he asked sarcastically. He had watched part of *Gone with the Wind* on HBO once. It had put him to sleep inside of twenty minutes. Of course, he'd been pretty drunk at the time.

They heard voices and looked around to see Casey walking up the path that led to the creek, talking animatedly to Ron Bouchoux, a slender, dark-haired local in his early twenties.

"Ron was just showing me his airboat, *Maringouin*," Casey said enthusiastically.

"Meringue what?" McKay demanded.

"*Maringouin*. Means mosquito, Billy. It's pretty far out. Looks like that baby can really *move*."

Casey had a great love of anything that went fast, particularly since his first love—flying fighter aircraft in combat—had gone unrequited for several years. After his famous five-kill mission had brought his shootdown total to seven, making him America's top scoring ace since the Korean War, he had been rotated home and virtually grounded, considered too valuable an asset to risk.

With his combination of natural aptitude, incredible eye, and laboriously acquired skill, he should have become an instructor at the Air Force's Aggressor air combat school. Instead he had wound up flying a desk at Vandenberg. He had always attributed that to the typical bureaucratic snafu. (Since he had barely been there three months when he was offered a chance to become a Guardian, McKay—knowing Major Crenna's propensity for working behind the scenes—wondered if that was true.) Though Casey had managed to get airborne a few times during his stint with the Guardians, even claiming a few new kills under some pretty incredible circumstances, it had been years since he'd known anything like the joy of flying his F-16.

Ron nodded eager agreement. "The back bayou, she's not worth so much; they twist around too much. But where you have the straight channel, or in the open marsh—ah, how she flies." He spoke with more than a hint of Cajun French accent, but at least McKay could understand him. Most of the people they'd met in the last couple of days spoke as if they had mouthfuls of mush, even the ones who didn't insist on speaking French half the time.

What was worse was that McKay actually spoke some French, and he *still* couldn't understand half of what the Acadians had to say.

They were arguing at the moment. "Don't mind them," Andres Daw said, standing to one side gnawing on a fried chicken leg. "They're always like this."

McKay grunted. He wasn't too happy about having to play it this way. On the other hand, the Guardians could hardly be expected to comb every square inch of the swamplands looking for what was certain to be a heavily concealed installation. And they didn't have much time: The backwater grapevine had confirmed the reports relayed to them via satellite from their Freehold friends, that the FSE team had landed several days before and begun sending out patrols in search of people to question.

"I think just about everybody's here," the guide said. "Anybody who matters, anyway."

McKay nodded. Even though Tom Rogers had been working on the locals from the time they started to filter in that afternoon, he figured he ought to make a bow in the direction of formality. "Gentlemen," he said, stepping up to the table. He didn't exactly shout, but the hubbub subsided instantly. He hadn't been a Parris Island drill instructor for nothing. "Thank you for coming. I'm Billy McKay. This is Casey Wilson, and Sam Sloan. I believe you've already met Tom Rogers. We're the Guardians, and we need your help."

A tall, heavyset old man, wearing of all things a white shirt and black string tie, rose and made a little formal speech of welcome—Auguste Falcon, their host, owner of the white house and brother-in-law of little Gariepy, who'd brought them here in his power boat and was sitting to one side as if trying to hide behind his luxuriant mustache. He was a gracious host, though McKay wondered cynically how much the good, solid gold the Guardians were passing out for assistance might have had to do with that.

He'd scarcely finished when a thick-shouldered, crew-cut man seated directly across from McKay shook his head and growled, "I don't even know why we're talking to these men. They're traitors."

McKay made a wolf sound in the thick of his throat and

leaned his weight onto his knuckles, pressing hard on the scarred wood of the table. Sam Sloan's fingers sank into his biceps like the jaws of a beartrap.

Flushed, old Falcon faced the man. "Mr. Charles, how can you say such a thing?"

"John Charles," Daw said softly in McKay's ear. "Hails from the Bayou Teche. Landowning family. Worked for the U.S. Attorney's office in Baton Rouge, back before the blowup."

Charles was glaring around at the others. He wasn't fat, but had the full-jowled features of a college linebacker gone to seed. "Doesn't anybody here listen to the radio? These men are wanted for treason by the United States Government."

"But I thought they were *from* the government," somebody said.

Trying to talk above a rising din, Charles said something about President Lowell. "But Mr. MacGregor, he is President," somebody else protested.

Charles hunched his heavy shoulders and glared around with exasperated gray eyes agleam in torchlight. "He's a damned traitor too. He seized the office of the President by trickery. Doesn't anybody here listen to KFSU?"

That brought silence. "*Non*," said a middle-aged man whom Ron had introduced as his father Joe Bouchoux. "We're all good Catholics here."

"Well, if you won't listen to me, just look at them, coming in here with that—that damned drug peddler."

"And good evening to you, too, Chuckles," Daw said dryly.

"Jeffrey MacGregor is the rightful President of the United States of America," Sam Sloan said, in his Steel Commander mode now, so cold and hard you expected to see condensation wisping off him. "He was held prisoner for a time by invaders from Europe—the same crew who are anchored down in Terrebonne. We rescued him."

"They're good American boys—"

"And Dutch, and German, and Belgian, and French—
and Russian, Mr. Charles. Some of them are indeed up-
standing men, who really believe they've come home to
help. But they're in the minority. Most of them came as
conquerers."

"We've heard what they've done," said a squint-eyed
man named Mattingly. "They stole everything that wasn't
nailed down or wrecked, over in Houston."

"But they are Americans," another man said. "I saw
them with my own eyes. Surely, they don't intend us any
harm. Why borrow trouble with them?"

"Ah, Camsell, you old fool, you're turning into an old
woman. They may be American, but they're under a foreign flag—"

The bugs were out in force, drawn by the torches.
McKay squashed a mosquito on the side of his neck, noted
with irritation that it had left a bright smear of blood across
his thumb. "They can go on like this all night," Daw said
softly.

"Are they gonna help?"

Daw showed tobacco-yellowed teeth. "Hard one to call.
You're asking a lot. The bottom line is, these FSE dudes
have a lot more guns than all these old muskrats put together, plus you guys."

McKay traded a bleak glance with Sloan. Even with the
help of the bayou folk, their chances of beating the Effsees
to Project Starshine didn't look any too bright. Without
their help, what chance did they have?

A shout from behind made them turn. A man in baggy
coveralls was trotting up the path that led past the single
tupelo tree to the little dock. "We've been invaded!" he
shouted.

"Old news, Pierre," Falcon said contemptuously.

"*Batiscan!*" the newcomer exclaimed. "Not that. It's the Cubans—the Cubans are in Atchafalaya Bay!"

"You know, McKay," Sloan said, "I think I've found a use for that eternal cigar of yours at last. It seems to help keep the bugs at bay."

"Yeah. They don't appreciate a good cigar. That's something you and them got in common."

Casey chuckled softly. They were distributed around the back stoop of Falcon's house, admiring the early-autumn constellations overhead. It was about two o'clock in the morning. Most of the men who had gathered for the conference were sacked out in bedrolls out front, beside the picnic table. The Guardians, favored guests, had been given two whole rooms from which old man Falcon's copious clan had been cleared. But they weren't ready to sleep yet.

"We got a problem," Rogers said softly. He sat on the steps with his wrists resting on his knees.

"Which one?" asked Casey, who lay full length on the planking with his head resting against a post.

"For starters, our local friends seem to be of far from one mind as to whether to give us a hand," Sloan pointed out.

"I don't blame them, man," Casey said. "They have two different armies parked on their doorsteps."

"Yeah," McKay said. "I think that's what Tom means by our problem."

"At least they don't, like, seem to be listening to that Charles dude. I think he wants them to string us up."

"So, Tom, to which of our multiplicity of problems were you referring?"

"We're going to have to arm and organize the people in the bayous," Rogers said.

Sloan blinked. "Are we getting ahead of ourselves?"

"I'm just sayin', it's something we're gonna have to do, if we want to pull this off."

"What do you mean?" Sam Sloan asked, taken aback. "You're not thinking of having the local people take on regular troops?"

"It's nothing we haven't done before, Sam," Casey remarked.

"We need to consider two possibilities, Sam," Rogers said softly. "First, the Effsees might find this Project Starshine before we do. Second—even if we find it first, they ain't going to stop looking. We have to do anything we can to deny it to them."

"Even if it means asking untrained fishermen and farmers to throw away their lives against heavily armed soldiers?" Sam almost shouted.

"Hey, take it easy," McKay grunted. "They ain't even agreed to help us look for Starshine yet."

Rogers faced the former naval officer calmly. "Yes."

For a moment Sloan's eyes held his. Then Sloan looked away. "You're right. But it's still kind of hard to take." He gave a small laugh. "But I think you're putting the cart before the horse, Tom. They haven't agreed to help us at all yet, let alone signed up to throw the Effsees into the Gulf of Mexico."

"What about these Cubans?" Casey asked.

McKay rubbed his jaw. "We're going to have to take a look at them. Maybe"—his cigar had burned down to a nub. He ground it out in the moist earth next to the footing —"maybe it could even be useful, having these Cubans on hand. Maybe—"

A shrill cry from the front yard cut him off. He snatched up his chopped M-60, which he had leaned up against the porch near to hand, raced around the side of the house with the other Guardians pounding behind him.

A tall, skinny Cajun dressed only in his skivvies stood pointing up at the sky while the other men gaped blearily from their bedrolls. "Look, there it is! There it is again."

Off to the west, moving slowly north to south a few degrees above the horizon, was an oval of bright yellow light. It looked like nothing Billy McKay had ever seen outside of a movie theater. "Holy shit," he breathed.

Beside him he felt Casey Wilson go tense, like a caged falcon watching a fat pigeon settling to the sidewalk outside his cage. Whatever it was, it was in his element of the sky, and he wanted to run it down, to find out what it was.

A babble of voices damped out the cricket songs. McKay thought he heard several men whisper, "*Wolf Bayou*," heard others firmly hush them. The light slid on into the north, eerily silent, and then was gone.

Pajama-clad, Colonel Enos Correy watched the light from the foredeck of the *Marshall*. The railing was lined with pointing, shouting men. "What I wouldn't give for a good Rapier air-defense system," he said aside to Myers, who stood by his side, still in his shirtsleeves.

"I'm sure the Chairman didn't feel our enemies had sufficient air capabilities to threaten us," the political officer said. His voice was not as steady as it might have been.

A naval officer appeared at the colonel's elbow, his crisp whites glowing like a will-'o-the-wisp in the starlight. "Captain's compliments, sir, and the bridge reports our radars can't pick it up, whatever it is."

"Maybe he's right," Correy said. "Maybe they don't."

CHAPTER
TEN —————————————

With swift, deft strokes, June-Marie paddled the pirogue along a clear channel through the drowned marshlands of the stub peninsula that separated Atchafalaya Bay from Terrebonne. Farther north, the land coalesced to some extent, held in place by roots of stands of willow and cypress and tupelo gum along the banks of classic bayous of the popular imagination. Here all was flat and treeless, random clear channels winding their way through the head-high weeds.

With a whir of wings, a fat lubber grasshopper landed on June-Marie's shirt and stood there cleaning its forelegs with its mandibles. Its jointed armor glinted like burnished metal in the early-morning sun. She didn't bother to brush it away. A girl who'd grown up in this country knew better than to fear harmless insects—particularly when there were things worth fearing in the wet country, from hairy

fishing spiders whose bite could raise itching lumps of in-
flammation, to the ever-present cottonmouths with their
poison-laden fangs. She let it ride as she paddled, stroke
after measured stroke in the slow green water, and pres-
ently it kicked away again to join one of its fellows
weighting down a long grass stem at channel's edge.

Once away from the house, she had made her way
blindly inland, her feet finding their own way to a hollow
in a thick strand of underbrush, in which she had often
spent the long eventless afternoons of her childhood. In
that green familiar womb, surrounded by the scents of
growth and wet earth, she had huddled for she did not
know how long, curled in a fetal knot. Most of the time,
blessedly, her mind had been blank with a strange dream-
less sleep.

At length she had awakened to what it took her some
minutes to realize was twilight. She stripped off her jeans,
examined herself by the dwindling gray light. Her belly
was still sore, and there was blood on her thighs in dried
patches like red lichen—she was no virgin, but the soldiers
had not been gentle. Still, as far as she could tell, no per-
manent damage was done. She washed herself, crawled
back into her covert, and slept through the night.

In the morning she had headed east. During her desperate, stumbling flight from her house, her thought had been
to flee to her brother—but she would not do that. She had
put that behind her, and she was damned if he would see
her humbled.

She had kinfolk living east, on Lake Raccourci—the
name meant *short-cut*—inland of the Casse-Tête Islands.
She had heard from them since the war, received an invitation to stay with them, passed along by the coasters and
swamp folk. She had chosen to remain behind in her own
family home, proud and self-sufficient. Now she shook her
head with a certain wry bitterness. *Self-sufficient. Well, I*

*was, I damned well was. It took a warship full of armed
men to drive me from my home—*

The passage widened with the juncture of another channel. Several spoonbills, summertime visitors to the marshlands, raised their heads from feeding as she passed. They
were tall, ungainly birds, perched on waders' long stiltlike
legs, pinkish-colored, their bills flat and flaring at the tip to
resemble their namesakes. Wet bits of grass dangled from
them like false mustaches. Their black eyes regarded her
with a total absence of curiosity or alarm. *Amazing how so
many creatures have lost their fear of man,* she thought.

When she'd awakened yesterday morning a curious
heavy calm had taken possession of her. Her first reasoned
thought had been to go and find her brother after all, not
out of panic, but to warn him of the presence of the
Cubans. The notion almost brought a smile. Luc would
find out about the Cubans soon enough, long before they
posed any threat to him. He had his ways.

It had been fortunate for her that she knew the location
of a small boat, hidden beneath a fallen bald cypress,
whose owner had not survived the plagues that followed
the war. The wetlands were difficult if not impossible to
traverse afoot, but she would far rather have used a
stranger's toothbrush than use a boat she came across without its owner's permission. Here in the coastal bayous,
where few roads had reached even before the war, life de-
pended on watercraft. Nor would she have had much success borrowing a boat. The thinly scattered population of
the area seemed sensibly to be making itself scarce.

Beneath the soft *plash* of the paddles she sensed a deep
hum—felt, rather than heard. She stopped, softly twisting
the paddle in the water to keep the needle-slim boat aligned
with the sluggish current. From a vibration in her bones the
sound rose to a thrum, took on a distinct staccato rhythm
that was abruptly all too familiar.

Helicopter! she thought wildly as the chopping sound rose around her like the wind. *Mother Mary, won't they let me be?*

She looked about frantically, knowing it was futile. Along the tree-lined bayou she could have made herself and her little boat invisible in the hammering heartbeats since she'd recognized the sound. Out here there was no cover but the reeds, and they offered no protection at all from aerial observation.

A moment and then she spotted it, south of her, and to her surprise she realized it was moving westward, toward Atchafalaya Bay. It was a Bell observation helicopter, sleek and green like a giant drab dragonfly, just like ones her brother had flown. She frowned. What was going on? She didn't think the Cubans used the same kind of helicopters as the U.S. Army.

She watched as it purred on into the west, oblivious to her presence. She continued to hear it after it vanished from sight. Puzzled, she began paddling again.

She'd made several hundred yards when she became aware of another sound. At first she took it for another helicopter, but it grew louder without differentiating itself into the quick beat of a helicopter's rotor. It was a curious sound, like nothing she had ever heard, a gusty mechanical roar, vaguely like the giant lawn-mower sound of an airboat's engine, but much deeper and fuller. Ahead and to the left she saw a flight of spoonbills taking wing like an explosion of confetti, voicing shrill alarm. Adrenaline stirred like a wild animal within her. Controlling it, she paddled toward the place from which the birds had lifted. Best she saw whatever this strange machine was before it spotted her.

The roaring filled her ears like the sound of a gulf storm, all-encompassing, so that if the flight of birds had not given her a clue, she would have had no idea where it originated. The little pirogue slid across the surface of the water as if frictionless, propelled by expert strokes as she worked her way toward it along the twisty channels.

It was upon her. She skimmed into a broad clear pool perhaps forty meters wide, and it came thundering through the reeds on the other side, a curious craft the size of a shrimp boat, held up by a bulging skirt of some kind of fabric, riding a dense roil of mud. She had a flashing impression of a turret squatting in front of a cabin topped with assorted masts, and then men crowded on the narrow gangway to either side of the cabin were pointing at her, faces making the motions of shouting words no one could hear over the awesome engine blast.

With one push of the paddle she had the craft broadside to the slow current, with a second she had it turned down a side channel, away from the great bellowing, diesel-reeking machine. She already knew it was too late, but it was no longer in her to give up without a struggle.

The engine howl fell to a rough idle that rattled in her bones as she scudded over the water. A moment later it roared into full volume again, then swelled further, faster, as if the bizarre contrivance was chasing her. It passed to her right. She shied from it, putting the sharp nose of her craft into the curtain of reeds to her left, parting them. She had to jump out for a moment to haul her boat across the bank of silt fixed by the roots of the plants, then she was rowing in the direction from which she had just come in a different passage.

The dragon-bellowing crossed her stern, came up on what was now her right. The beast had attempted to head her off, misjudged her speed and overshot her. She allowed herself a moment of hope. Even though the hovercraft could travel much more quickly than she, and didn't need to restrain itself to the passages between banks of reeds, with a little luck it could blunder around in this marsh all day and never stumble across her. In time the crew would lose interest—how important could she be, a single woman in a tiny boat? *Surely they can find victims to rape more easily,* she thought bitterly.

The clamor passed across her bow. Almost at once it settled back into its loud idle. Frowning, she steered her boat along a passage that twisted to her right. What was going on? The hovercraft's cabin wasn't elevated high enough to spot her at any distance among these reeds, and even if they were foolish enough to think she was in some sort of power boat they'd never hear any engine noise above the blast of their own fans, even on idle.

It suddenly came clear to her what her pursuers were doing in the split second before a man came wading out of the reeds scant meters to her left. He was wearing American issue OD battledress with an unfamiliar insignia sewn on the right shoulder. He carried an M-16. He shouted, barely audibly even this distance from the hovercraft, lunged to grab her gunwale. She hacked at him savagely with the paddle. He let go with a curse and fell backward, thrashing the water while she tried to straighten the small boat, which had already slid broadside to the current.

Ten meters ahead a second soldier appeared, wading out to block the eight-foot-wide passage. She dropped her oar behind her in the boat and reached for something resting in the prow, between her feet parallel to the long axis of the craft. It was a Bear composite bow, strung and ready—even with its waterproof nylon string, a far from ideal weapon for the bayou country, wet and choked with dense entangling underbrush, but it had been the only weapon left to her, when she fled her house, that she had any idea of how to use. The bow was her brother's. He had been an archery enthusiast since early youth, and had taught her a lot. For some reason he hadn't taken the bow and its waterproof case with him to his new haven. She grabbed it up, nocked an arrow, drew and let fly while the soldier was still waving his hands at her.

He stopped and stared stupidly down at the shaft sticking out, several centimeters to the right of his breastbone. His knees went. His coal-scuttle helmet slipped off to reveal closely cropped brick-red hair. He half turned, so she could see sunlight winking off the razor edges of the steel broadhead protruding from his back. Then he pitched over on his side in the water as she frantically paddled past him.

Too late. They were closing in on her from all directions, their shouts so close she could hear them easily above the hovercraft's roar. Several spilled out into the channel in front of her, floundering, raising great ungainly splashes, but blocking her passage. When they saw their comrade lying in the water with the arrow through him, several raised their weapons.

A black man's voice rapped orders, and the weapons came down. Then she was surrounded by a half-dozen men, fending off her paddle swings with their rifles, grabbing her arms and hauling her out of the boat to stand in the waist-deep water. She felt the strength ebbing from her like blood from a slashed wrist, dropped to her knees so the brackish water came up to her breasts, and wept.

"All right, tie her up, stick her back in the boat, and bring her," Sergeant Gates ordered. "Not too tightly, dammit. Shee-it, I can't hardly hear myself *think*, for that damned blower."

"She shot Willy," Private Luttrell said. His almost-white hair was falling in his eyes beneath the brim of his helmet. "He looks pretty bad."

The sergeant grimaced. "So get him patched up and put him in the boat too. Them arrows ain't got much shocking power. He don't bleed to death, he ought to be okay." For all his years on the firing line, Gates still took it personally when one of his men got hurt. Still, who could blame the girl? She had to be scared half-crazy.

"Why'd she shoot him, Sarge?" Luttrell persisted.

"Yeah, why'd she run away?" demanded Madlock, a tall, rawboned swamper from Georgia with a lynx's yellow eyes. "I bet she's some kind of spy."

Several of the platoon were now binding the unresisting woman's arms behind her with some of the nylon restraints they'd been issued for these patrol sweeps. Others tended to the injured man.

"She was scared. That's why she shot him. That's all."

"Then why were we in such an all-fired hurry to chase her down?"

"Because we got ordered to drive around in this here swamp and bring back anybody we run into."

Another troopie splashed up. "Sergeant, the medic says we better leave the arrow in Willy at least until we get him back to the ACV."

"Awright. Stick him in the boat—"

"Sergeant," called Private Sanchez, wading up to join the little group. As always he was stooped way over like a little old man, so everybody would know how heavily the radio weighed him down.

"What do you *want*, Sanchez?" Gates asked the round-faced commo man.

Sanchez tapped the lightweight foam earpiece of the headset he wore beneath his helmet. "Maczurek says to get back to the blower on the double. They got some kind of riot in Cocodrie, and they want all units back there right now!"

Sam Sloan pursed his lips and whistled. "Take a look at *that*. A Krivak II missile frigate, as I live and breathe. From her number she's the former *Razitelny*—currently

doing business as *Cienfuegos,* pride of the Cuban Navy."
He shook his head. "I thought she was lost when we
bombed the bases in Cuba, when the balloon was going
up."

"Give me a look," Andres Daw said. Sloan passed him
the glasses.

"She looks *big,*" Ron Bouchoux said breathlessly.

Gnawing on his underlip and humming to himself,
Sloan nodded. "Not by the standards of the old days—
she's just a hair over four hundred feet long, hardly a lifeboat compared to, say, the old *Nimitz*-class carriers. But
pretty damned big for this era of diminished expectations."
He shook his head. "What a beauty. The Krivaks always
were handsome ships."

Daw's ugly face was expressionless as a polished cypress knee. "Looks heavily armed," he grunted.

"No kidding. She's got two one-hundred-millimeter
guns in her aft turrets, eight each twenty-one-inch torpedo tubes, a couple of twelve-barreled RBU 6000 anti-
submarine projectors, and for good measure a couple of
twin SA-N-4 surface-to-air missile launchers."

"What about those things on her bows, look like six
skinny boilers stacked up three and three?"

Sloan showed his teeth. *"That's* the main event:
launchers for SS-N-23 ship-killing missiles. Soviet copies
of the French Advanced Exocet—the new generation of
the missile that gave the British so much trouble in the
Falklands War. She packs one hell of a punch."

Daw lowered the glasses and curled his lip. "Yeah. And
here we sit in a rowboat."

Sloan laughed. It was perfectly true. And, now that the
smuggler-turned-guide mentioned it, it did make him feel
mighty vulnerable, sitting here in a rowboat with that sleek
nautical killer lying not five hundred meters away and
nothing but a screen of reeds for protection.

The sky was darkening toward dusk, the water lying calm and leaden under a few clouds. A multitude of sea-birds dodged and shrieked their raucous calls overhead; in the bayous behind, the nightbirds would just be coming out, working great destruction on the insects that rose in clouds from the water. Sloan felt a sudden hankering for the protection of the cypress swamp; he of all people knew what those potent missiles could do to a ship. Cruder ones than those poised in their launching tubes in the A position on the frigate's deck had damned near sunk the *Winston-Salem* beneath him.

Sloan and his party had left the morning after the confab at the Falcon house. There had been a certain amount of debate as to who should go. Billy McKay, of course, had insisted on going himself. Tom Rogers had set him straight on that one. Aside from continuing the search for Star-shine, the Guardians had to try to talk the bayou people into helping them do something about the Effsee expedition—and, toughest of all, try to come up with some plan that might have some result other than the inevitable mas-sacre of civilians by several hundred trained troops. Billy McKay was the last man who could be spared.

Tom Rogers couldn't go either—if anyone could scoop together a force that would give the Effsees grief, it was the former Green Beret. That left Sam and Casey; and since, if there were actually Cubans in Atchafalaya Bay, they would pretty well have had to come by ship, Navy man Sloan seemed the logical choice to go scope them out, assess what kind of threat they posed.

McKay had been visibly unhappy with the prospect of sending Sloan off by himself. But there wasn't much choice. If anything broke, McKay was going to need as many Guardians as he could get to handle the situation. So Sam went off on this reconnaissance trip, with Daw for a guide and young Bouchoux to get them where they needed to go. Sloan felt offended by his leader's lack of confidence in him at the same time that he felt a certain trepidation. It was McKay and Rogers who were expert at this sort of work. He wasn't afraid to die, but he had a deathly fear of fucking up.

Daw and Ron knew the area between Atchafalaya and Terrebonne Bay south of the Intracoastal Waterway the way they knew their own reflections in the mirror. Driving his airboat with an abandon that put Sam uncomfortably in mind of Casey Wilson, Ron had boomed them down Bayou du Large to Lake Mechant, west across the lake, then into a tangle of bayous which, by a series of twists and turns Sam had no hope of ever remembering, brought them to within ten kilometers of the point where Four League Bay met Atchafalaya Bay before nightfall.

That was as far as they dared take the airboat. Beyond that, there was too much chance of their quarry hearing the noise of an engine.

They spent the night in hammocks stretched between cypress boles, listening to the crickets and the bullfrogs and the booming of the gators. Sloan draped himself with mosquito netting. When he woke to Daw's big hand shaking him awake, he knew at once it hadn't done much good.

They breakfasted on perch Ron caught and set out rowing in a little dinghy. Sloan didn't know how Daw knew where to find the boat, didn't reckon it was his business. What had been his business was helping to row the damned thing. The fact that they were only about six miles from their objective as the crow flew didn't make much difference; crows didn't lay out bayous.

It had taken them almost all day. The quirky bayou currents often seemed to Sloan to flow in apparent defiance of the laws of gravity, or as often against them as with them; fortunately they were on the slow side. By the time they reached the dubious protection of the reed marsh fringing the bay, Sloan was exhausted, and pretty well sunburned despite the protection of sunscreen and a boonie hat.

Once they'd had a look at the frigate, they sculled around a little until they caught sight of a small assortment of tents ashore. There wasn't much sign of activity. "What can they be doing?" Ron wondered.

"Probably standing in to make repairs," Daw said. "She's probably been a long time out of drydock."

"You're right."

"Have you seen enough, or would you like to admire the ship a little longer?"

Sloan slapped his arm. "The bugs are getting aggressive again. We might as well head back while we've got at least some light."

They turned the boat around. It wallowed gently, making soft sloshing sounds that had a lulling effect on the exhausted Sloan, notwithstanding the menacing presence of the frigate. "It would be nice to just spend some time in this country," he remarked. "It has a real beauty to it. Serenity—except for these damned bugs."

"Wait till you see a hurricane come up. *Then* you won't think it's so damned peaceful," Daw said.

Behind him Ron's oar froze in the water. "Listen," he whispered.

Daw and Sloan frowned at each other. Then Daw lifted his heavy face to the eastern sky. "That's a helicopter."

"Uh-oh," Sloan said. "Sounds like the Effsees have come to take a look at our friends in the frigate."

"*Merde,*" Ron said with feeling. He started to paddle hard.

Daw shook his head. "They get a look at that thing, they're not going to bother with us."

A klaxon raised its spastic whooping-crane cry from the

frigate. The decks suddenly came alive with mostly shirt-less seamen running this way and that. "Will their SAMs take out a helicopter?" Daw asked.

"I have a feeling we're about to find out," Sloan said.

"Holy Mary, Mother of God."

Sloan looked at Ron, who'd produced the strangled whispered exclamation. The kid was pointing off into the northeast. An ovoid of yellow light was gliding across the sky out of the north, toward the bay.

"It's the saucer," Ron breathed.

At that point the chopper jockey either noticed the UFO or decided that an obvious warship the size of the one lying in Atchafalaya Bay was certain to have antiaircraft capability. Probably both. The helicopter pivoted beneath its main rotor and darted back toward the east. The whine of its engines took on a higher timbre.

A line of green light, fantastically intense, connected UFO with fleeing helicopter for the tiniest fraction of a second. The chopper blew up in a spatter of glowing fragments of molten metal, followed in half a second by the explosion of its fuel and munitions stocks. An astringent crack reached the ears of the stunned men in the boat, then the double boom of the helicopter exploding as debris and flaming fuel rained down on the distant patch of swamp.

"Holy shit," Sam said.

The glowing ovoid was hovering, appearing to observe its handiwork. The wreckage finished falling out of the sky. Without appearing to turn, the unknown craft moved back north again. There was a blue-white flash and a SAM shrieked away from its launcher on the frigate, drawing a dense line of white smoke behind it that caught the light of the dying sun and glowed pink against the mauve sky. The missile failed to track, passing almost directly over the three men in the boat to bury itself in some inland bayou. The UFO didn't even deign to take evasive action.

"I think we'd better be getting back now," Andres Daw said in a more subdued tone than Sloan had ever heard him use.

"I think you're right," Sam said with feeling.

CHAPTER
ELEVEN ─────────────────

Political Officer Myers blinked at Colonel Correy with his pale schoolmaster's eyes. "I don't really have to answer to you, you know," he said.

Correy's face was clenched, his tan almost whited out with anger. "I've got two men dead and seven injured. I don't even want to think about how many locals were killed or hurt. I'm entitled to an explanation, and I'm damned well going to get one."

Myers flicked his eyes about the cabin. At the moment the only chair in the spartan little office was the one behind the desk, occupied by a very angry Colonel Correy. *Very well, let him play his little game.* He leaned his lanky frame against the door.

"Since you're going to take that tack, Colonel, perhaps you might do me the favor of explaining what it is *I'm* supposed to explain."

Correy thrust his lower jaw forward like a bulldog setting his teeth in a steer's ear. Myers folded his arms. "You know damned well what I'm talking about," the colonel growled.

"No, no I don't, frankly."

"Perhaps it slipped your attention that the populace of the little town of Cocodrie pitched a riot this afternoon. There was a lot of shooting—"

"Now, that was the result of a very unfortunate oversight on the part of your officers, permitting the locals to retain firearms."

"We are not here to shake down the local inhabitants. We're here to find a secret Buck Rogers power plant of some sort. We can't go searching people's houses without good reason. We're not an invading army. This is America, dammit, and we're Americans."

Sadly the political officer looked at Correy. *He's a good man, really a good man, but how little he understands of some matters.*

"Well," he said, "it was an unfortunate incident. But I have every confidence that from now on, your men will take the measures necessary to keep the populace in line—"

"What the riot was about," Correy overrode him, "was the fact that your Special Police have been borrowing townspeople and neglecting to return them. I find that, without consulting me, your men have been bringing people back to the ship and interrogating them. I'm even given to understand that there are a number of such captives unaccounted for. That's why the locals rioted. That's why I have men dead and injured."

"I understand that your casualties deeply concern you, Colonel. It's a mark of your worthiness as an officer. But casualties are an inevitable part of this business. Like that poor kid today, shot with an arrow, or the crew of the recon chopper . . . " He shook his head and grinned a Will Rogers grin. "Would you believe it, a lot of the enlisted men are saying that so-called flying saucer shot the chopper?"

"That's just loose talk. Choppers are tricky beasts; accidents happen." The colonel's blunt fingers brushed a breast pocket of his immaculate uniform blouse. Myers recalled that he had given up smoking a year before, according to his dossier. Apparently he felt a certain deep-seated inclination to revert to the addiction in times of stress. Another piece of data to file away.

"But let's not wander away from the subject, Political Officer," Correy continued. "Just how do you justify starting a riot with your unauthorized abduction and Gestapo tactics?"

Myers pushed off from the wall, took three short steps, all the limited space permitted. "Duty compels me to remind you once again that I don't have to answer to you, Colonel—just for the record. I don't really want to pull rank on you, as it were. But just as you have your area of responsibility on this mission, so have I."

He held up a widely spread hand to fend off an outburst. The colonel's face had turned a dangerous purplish color, and the scars stood out white and stark as chalk stripes. "But I'll be more than happy to tell you what does justify my actions, Colonel. In a word, results."

The tendons were standing out in relief from Correy's thick neck. With an effort he bit back whatever it was he intended to say, then blinked and stared up at the political officer through lowered brows. "Results? What are you talking about?"

"I mean we've found it, Colonel. We know the location of Project Starshine."

Correy sagged back in his chair as if sandbagged.

"That's impossible," he croaked.

Lips pursed, Myers shook his head. "If I didn't know you, Colonel, I'd be strongly tempted to suspect you doubted the wisdom of our Chairman in sending us on this mission, to hear you talk like that. But let's not worry about that. The important thing is, I—we—have found the facility. It lies in Wolf Bayou, in the Atchafalaya Swamp."

For a moment Correy could do nothing but sit there and stare at the white half-moons of his cuticles. He could think of nothing to say. Finally, he cleared his throat. "This is unbelievable. Just how did you find this out, anyway?"

Myers made an easy gesture. "Oh, it's nothing special. Just a process of deduction. Sherlock Holmes stuff. We ascertained that there was a region everybody's afraid of. I mean *everybody*, the people in the town, the people who've been interviewed out in the bayous. Everyone we mention the subject to expresses a fear of the place. They tell crazy stories about what goes on there. It's supposed to be lousy with plague, and things a lot worse than that. Supernatural stuff. That UFO is supposed to be seen going in and out of there all the time; none of the natives will willingly go near the place."

"What the hell does that have to do with anything?" Correy demanded in a voice like a rasp being drawn over angle iron.

"Well, shucks, Colonel, everything. Just think about it: what better way to hide a secret facility? Before the war, they could benefit from the fact that the Atchafalaya Basin is still sparsely populated, with a lot of it set aside for game preserves, that sort of thing. But after the war, when people are going to be, let's face it, a lot less scrupulous about preserving the sanctity of our wilderness areas and whatnot—what better way to make people keep their distance than by somehow spreading all kinds of wild rumors among these fundamentally superstitious bayou folk?"

Correy rubbed his cheek. "It sounds pretty farfetched," he said thoughtfully.

"Think about it, Colonel. Doesn't it all add up?"

"Yeah. Yeah, maybe it does at that." He shook his head. "I've got to admit that beyond this we haven't got lead one as to where the damned facility is."

He sat there frowning and cogitating. Myers said nothing. He most particularly wanted to avoid saying anything that might tilt the colonel's mind back to the question of the unauthorized detentions and questionings. Because some of Myers's Special Police operatives had been a bit out of line, had been a bit more vigorous with some of the detainees than might have strictly been called for—nothing that could be left at Myers's own door, of course; but still, to bruit the subject about unnecessarily might lead the colonel into making statements that the political officer might have to take official note of.

Particularly since the Special Police interrogations, comprehensive as they were, had had nothing to do with solving the mystery. People weren't happy to talk about Wolf Bayou, but they made no secret of fearing it. Myers had drawn his inferences from that fact. Which, if the colonel's attention was drawn to it, might just lead him to think Special Police methods had unnecessarily caused today's incident. And that could be an unfortunate conclusion all the way around.

Correy rapped his knuckles on his palm. "I can't say you've sold me on this, Myers. But I can't say you might not have something here. Tomorrow we'll see about sending a team over into the Atchafalaya to visit this Wolf Bayou of yours and see what there is to see."

"Great. I'm confident this will all work out, quite confident." He opened the door, started out, then stopped and turned back. "By the way, Colonel, I think you come down a little too hard on my Specials. But I've got some of them out tonight on a little hunting expedition. We got a very intriguing bit of local intelligence just today, and if there's anything to it—"

He grinned boyishly. "Just let me say it could be very interesting."

Sam sat in the bow of the airboat with his Galil/M-203 combo across his knees. He was bleary with fatigue, and the omnipresent humid swamp heat.

"Sam Sloan to Guardians, Sam Sloan to Guardians, come in please Guardians." For probably the third time in the last ten minutes he tried subvocalizing for his personal communicator again. He had taken it out of his pocket and fiddled with the gain and the tuning for a few minutes, but there was only so much he could do in the dark, without tools—and with devil-may-care Ron Bouchoux slapping the airboat across the surface of Lake Mechant with what Sloan thought was unnecessary exuberance.

Admit it, it's hopeless. They're still much too far out of range. He felt strange, very vulnerable, to have the umbilicus that tied him to his comrades severed. Usually at least one of his teammates was on watch in Mobile One, whose sophisticated receivers with their computer-driven filters and other technological wonders could pick up the transmissions of the Guardians' calculator-sized radios reliably at a range of a hundred kilometers. But Mobile One herself was a good twenty klicks upstream of the Guardians, unless for some reason or another they had returned to her. And that was too much of a coincidence to hope for.

He realized they were approaching an apparently solid wall of cypress trees at a breakneck pace. He steeled himself, damned if he was going to play the city slicker intimidated into protesting Ron's handling of the boat. Still that black, apparently solid wall hurtled closer, and Sloan couldn't help imagining what driving into the bole of a tree at this speed might do to the boat and its occupants. Even clipping a cypress knee could have pretty spectacular results.

He had just turned halfway around, mouth opened to protest, when he saw the glitter of starlight on water in a bayou's mouth dead ahead. At the same instant Ron throttled back with the flick of a practiced wrist. The airboat's blunt prow settled back toward the horizontal, and Sloan let out a deep breath.

"The Delormes have a cabin just up this bayou," Ron shouted, bending forward in hopes of making himself heard. His accent wasn't made any easier to decipher by the whine of the airboat's engine. "I thought we might spend the night here on the way back. But I think we need to get back too much, so instead we just stop for the fuel —if that is okay with you?"

Sloan's tailbone felt as if somebody had been hammering on it—and come to think of it somebody had; the plain plank seating in the airboat wasn't padded, and it had a tendency to jackhammer against his rump when crossing the wind-rippled surface of the lake. And he was exhausted—only adrenal terror at the prospect of what would happen to him if he slacked his grip and fell out of the damned boat was keeping him upright. But he would no more think of stopping now to rest than he would of writing a fan letter to Chairman Maximov. He had to get word back to McKay and the rest about the Cuban frigate and the bizarre downing of the FSE helicopter.

The huge fan at the rear of the boat slowed, and Ron steered the craft into the bayou at a pace that was almost sedate. As the silent walls of vegetation closed in to either side, bending low to dangle long moss tails in the slow-rolling water, Sloan belatedly recognized, or thought he did, the channel that cut between the lake and Bayou du Large. After a couple of minutes he decided any pretense of knowing where he was was sheer bravado. The damned bayous all looked alike after dark. He didn't see how it was possible either the guide or the youthful driver could have any idea where they were going, but he didn't think it would be tactful to display his uncertainty.

Sure enough, in no time at all the airboat was nuzzling a root-twined bank like an affectionate dolphin, and here was a little landing built of rough-dressed boards, steps leading up to a cabin built on stilts, partially out over the water. Daw got out first. Sam followed him up the rickety-feeling steps, glad to be stretching his legs after so many hours of sitting in the boat.

"Are you sure anybody's home?" whispered Sloan.

Daw turned back to him as he reached the deck. Before he could say anything a spotlight stabbed down from the pitched roof of the cabin, pinning them in blue-white glare.

"All right, you assholes, *freeze!*" a voice shouted in darkness.

Quick as a mongoose Daw ripped his revolver out of his holster, whipped around and fired. The spotlight shattered and died. From the house blossomed the muzzle-blast of a heavy shotgun. Daw grunted as the charge took him in the chest. Miraculously he didn't fall, instead raised his pistol and fired two shots in the direction of the blast. A scream answered him, then a volley of shots, seeming to be coming from within the darkened house and the woods to both side.

Daw went down. "Ron!" Sam screamed. "Run like hell —go tell the others—"

Clamping the stock of his Galil to his side with his elbow, he cut off his own words with a ripping burst. The muzzle flashes illuminated men in dark uniforms pouring out of the house and onto the landing from the undergrowth to both sides. Several went down as the needle-sharp 5.56 rounds ripped through them.

Shots were cracking past him at such a clip that they sounded like a flag snapping in a smart breeze. "Don't hurt him, you assholes," he heard somebody yell. "Take him alive!"

He turned to dive off the landing to the water eight feet below. A hand grabbed his arm. He pivoted, buttstroked a clean-shaven jaw, thanking God his stock was decent wood and not plastic from Mattel.

Cursing, grunting, sweating men surrounded him. More hands grabbed his rifle. Behind him he heard the airboat engine fire up with an angry snarl. It howled away from the pier while dark-uniformed men sprayed fire after it from long rifles.

Somebody slugged him from behind with the butt of an FN. It wasn't plastic either.

The boat cruised along the bayou propelled by a tiny outboard engine. It wasn't much if any louder than that of the fancy inflatable assault boats the Guardians had trucked down in Mobile One. Billy McKay sat in the bow, half-uneasy that the craft's design compelled him to sit with his back facing in the direction of travel, half-glad for the opportunity to admire his driver.

Word of the riot in Cocodrie had diffused rapidly through the bayou country in a dozen tendrils of rumor, each of which stung like the tentacle of a Portuguese man-of-war. Noncommittal before, the bayou folk were now edgy, angry, and looking for trouble. The FSE force had gone from being potential friends to actual invaders in a blink of their eyes.

McKay didn't even have a clear picture of what had happened, or what was supposed to have happened. When he factored out the usual bloodbath exaggerations, it didn't come up sounding like that big of a deal. What the hell? Occupying forces always trolled in people to interrogate, and generally didn't offer too many apologies for that or anything else they did.

"Shoot, Billy," Rogers had told him when he expressed surprise, "these're *Americans*. They don't know nothing about being occupied. That's why they're so touchy."

For a moment the former Green Beret had stared off past McKay's shoulder. Then he almost smiled. "I kind of thought our friends the Effsees would oblige us by pulling some kinda trick like this. Just didn't reckon they'd get around to it so soon."

So Casey had gone off north on a flying foray to Mobile One, and McKay had gone off to a meeting of some of the main men, clan heads and like that, at a house a few klicks away. Rogers stayed home at the Falcon house to talk with certain contacts he'd made in the last several days. McKay suspected that the men who were actually going to be instrumental in any kind of campaign against the FSE expeditionary force were meeting with Rogers, but *he* was going off to a bitch session by a lot of old coots who, once they had given their go-ahead for the whole thing, would mostly sit around on their front porches muttering in their whiskers about how they'd have done everything so much better when *they* were young.

McKay was right on target, at least so far as he was concerned. Now he was headed back, trying to ignore the horrible furnace heat that seemed to pour down from the sky to be reflected back by the water, and trapped by the encroaching greenery at just about the level of the boat. And taking advantage of the sole compensation offered for an otherwise wasted morning.

"And just what the hell are you staring at?" his driver demanded with a trace of the ubiquitous Acadian accent.

McKay shifted his rump on the unyielding plank. "What do you think I'm staring at?" He longed ferociously for a beer.

She sniffed. Her name was Jeannette Robidoux, Jenny for short, and she was well worth looking at. She was five foot two, hardly up to McKay's breastbone, her skin smooth and tan and stretched taut over a figure that managed to be wiry as a tigress while being nicely filled out in what, as far as McKay was concerned, were all the right places. She had amber hair, streaked with sunfading, not very long and gathered at the back of her neck by a rubber band, with a John Deere cap pulled down over it. Her face was an oval sharply pointed at the bottom, with wide cheekbones, narrow nose, eyes that were long and green and slightly slanted, and that flashed angrily at him before looking pointedly elsewhere. She had on a man's bush jacket that she didn't bother to button all the way to her throat, salmon-colored shorts, a pair of white tennis shoes from K-mart. She looked like something from one of those trashy B swamp-action flicks that Joe Bob Briggs was always telling his readers to check out at the drive-ins.

McKay fished out a cigar and lighter from a breast pocket of his cammie coveralls, which he'd unzipped to his navel. "Don't light that!" the girl hissed at him.

He raised an eyebrow. "What, is the No Smoking sign lit?"

"The smell of smoke. You don't know how far it will carry."

He started to protest about the sound of the engine carrying, realized that muffled and throttled down as it was, it wouldn't carry very far at all with all these damned trees and bushes and spooky moss for soundproofing.

"So who the hell is going to smell it?"

A shrug. "Who knows? Better not take the chance."

McKay was getting very hot under the collar, and it wasn't just from this Bessemer-process bayou. He was a man who prided himself on his bushcraft, and this snide little twat was showing him up. "No Effsee is going to penetrate this far without your people spotting them and passing the word."

"That's probably true. But aren't you taking a lot for granted, trusting us to be so alert? You hardly know us. And if there were enemies on the bayou, how would they get the word to us?"

He just sat there, feeling like his ass had just turned to lead and maybe his head, too. A little late into the game, he realized she was jacking with him—but she had a point, too. And their super state-of-the-art communicators, which so far had been a thousand more times reliable than any field radios he'd ever known, had been giving them fits in this damned swamp.

"How do you know all this, anyway?"

"My daddy raised me up a poacher," she said sweetly.

"Don't let Sam Sloan hear you say that. He's liable to snap back to his Sierra Club days and take a potshot at you."

"Commander Sloan would do no such thing. He's a perfect gentleman."

He looked down at the cigar in his hand, broke it in two and threw it into the coffee-colored water. "There. I'm a litterbug. Arrest me." He scooped up his M-60E3 and laid it across his lap. He looked alertly from side to side, to give his eyes somewhere to go other than roaming Jenny's taut little bod.

"I'll bet you think you look just like Sylvester Stallone with that big gun," she remarked.

He felt his face turn red. "Lady, I do not look one damned bit like Sylvester Stallone." Privately, he liked to think he looked more like Jim McMahon, who used to be quarterback for the Bears. Maybe not *quite* as pretty.

They rode on that way, McKay sulking, Jeannette calm and cheerful as if she were going for a Sunday outing, not even having the decency to work up a sweat. Fortunately it wasn't far to the Falcon landing. The boat bumped along-side and McKay got out, thanking his lucky stars that one thing he did know was how to deass watercraft without looking like a bozo; one false move and the little bitch would hoot him clear to Houston.

He felt no overwhelming urge to offer her a hand up. She popped out like a shorebird, made the boat fast to the ancient dock, then started up the path leading up the low hummock to the big old white house. As she passed McKay she gave him a slap on the ass.

He gaped after her as she walked on, never looking at him, swaying her own tight little ass up the pathway. "Son of a *bitch*," he muttered.

"Billy?" Tom Rogers's voice said instantly in his ear.

"I hear you, Tom."

"We been trying to get you all morning. Somebody blew our recon party. Sam's been captured."

CHAPTER
TWELVE —————————————

The interrogation room had clearly been an office, with its neat little desk and cubbyhole file on the wall behind. With morbid fascination, June-Marie searched the drab carpet and white-painted walls for signs of blood. She couldn't find any. She wasn't much reassured.

The chief interrogator leaned back in his swiveled chair behind the desk, cocked an elbow onto the chair's back. His pale gray shirt was open at the collar. The cut of his trousers and the midnight-blue jacket hung from a hook on the wall behind him, like the uniforms of the two men who stood silently behind June-Marie's chair, looked more police than military.

"Well, sweetheart, do you have anything more to say to us this morning?" he asked. He was young, middle twenties perhaps, about the same as June-Marie. He was of medium height, tan, with brown hair bleached almost to blond by the sun. He had a long lip and a short nose, looked very slightly like a juvenile Steve McQueen. He had the firm-fleshed boisterousness of a college jock.

Wordlessly, June-Marie shook her head. This was her third interview since she had been bundled aboard the large white ship yesterday. In neither of the previous sessions had she been physically abused, though her interrogators had gotten red in the face and shouted at her a lot.

In fact, she'd been pretty well treated: she had a little tiny cabin—or stateroom, or whatever you called them—to herself, down on the lower decks, with its own little bathroom and everything, though it was a little too close to the never-silent engines whose turning kept the ship supplied with power. So attuned was she to wild-animal caution that her first reaction to the quarters had been fear. It put her in mind of the old saying, *the condemned ate heartily,* of the way the government would nurse an injured felon assiduously back to health, so he would be in good shape to go to his death in the electric chair.

When she calmed down, she realized that the ship was simply so big, with the bulk of the troops ashore, that there was no point in not giving her her own cabin. In fact, from what she had seen of the activity ashore, she guessed that even when everyone was aboard there would still have been room left over. It was a far cry from the stories her brother had told her of troopships—but then again, whoever had sent these men probably didn't have near as many soldiers as the United States used to.

It hadn't been the U.S. Government, she was sure, for all that most of her captors were Americans. There were too many foreign accents, and the flags they flew were alien: a blue map of Europe enclosed in a blue circle, on a field of white, the same as their shoulder patches.

She'd even had a mess steward or whatever they called them, a skinny kid in white with yellow hair and prominent ears and a British accent, bring her a tray at mealtimes. His first visit had reawakened fears of being pampered for the noose, but then she settled down again and figured out that they had to feed her somehow, and this was easier than escorting her to a commissary.

She spoke to the boy on his first visit, asking him to try and get a message to the soldier she had shot, saying that she hoped he would recover. He gulped and nodded and left, and June-Marie didn't know whether the word would get through or not.

She didn't regret shooting the man—that had been necessity. But after the fact she bore him no ill will. He had only been doing his duty. To her surprise, some time after she judged the sun had gone down, there was a knock at her cabin door, and who should it be but the black sergeant in charge of the squad that captured her, to tell her that the injured boy would recover just fine and had said to tell her there were no hard feelings. The sergeant said he was sorry that they had frightened her, hoped she would be released soon, and bade her good night.

So there were real men among these curious soldiers, obvious Americans who wore alien insignia. Then there were the others—like the fit young man smirking across his desk at her.

He leaned forward, resting a forearm on the desk. "Nothing to say?" The words carried a riding-crop flick of menace.

"I told you," she said listlessly, "I was trying to reach family I have, over to Barataria—"

He cut her off. "I know, I know. After the Cubans ran you out." She had given him a truthful but heavily edited account of her experiences. The whole truth was much too personal . . . especially for the likes of him.

"She's lying, Lieutenant," one of the gorillas standing behind her growled.

The officer leaned back, steepling fingers in front of his chest. "You know what I think, honey? I think you're a fucking spy."

She looked at him.

He snorted laughter. "You think you're pretty tough, huh, honey? Well, I'll tell you something. You're shit, just like the rest of your peckerwood swampers." She felt the skin on her face grow taut. She fought to keep her emotions from becoming visible—she wouldn't give this *canaille* the satisfaction.

He frowned a bit at her lack of response, leaned back again. "Still think you're something? I tell you, babe, we could have you crying for your momma in no time flat. But we won't. You know why? Because we don't need to.

"You coonasses thought you could keep your precious Wolf Bayou secret from us. But we"—he tapped himself on the chest—"we worked it out anyway."

The voice went on, an arrogant wasp's drone. She could no longer hear the words for the roaring in her ears. *Wolf Bayou!* How could they have learned? The name meant nothing to the people hereabouts, only as a symbol of superstitious dread.

Luc! I've got to get away, got to warn him—

With a heave of her spirit she controlled herself again. The jock was still gloating at her, oblivious to the shock he'd given her, and she felt contempt for his skills as an interrogator. An able man would have spotted the flicker of reaction at the name *Wolf Bayou,* had her dead to rights.

"—but maybe it would be a different story if our esteemed colonel had balls in his pants," the man was saying, too absorbed with himself to pay attention to her. "If it was one of *us* you'd shot, PO Myers would give you quite a sendoff, I promise you that."

"Correy's a fucking namby-pamby," the other man behind her said. "He ought to let us teach these swampers to get uppity."

"I don't know what you're talking about," she said levelly.

The interrogator shook his head. "Do you guys believe this? Is this bitch too dumb to live, or what?" He sneered at her. "We know everything, baby, and I mean everything. We even know you've got the fucking Guardians backing you up in the swamps somewhere. Well, let me tell you, if you think they're going to haul your pretty little ass out of this fire, you've got it all wrong. We caught one of the bastards not long after we caught you, and it won't be long until we scoop up the rest."

She looked down at the faded knees of her jeans. *The Guardians! Why would the President's special bodyguards be here? It must have to do with the Project, it has to!* Her muscles knotted with frustration and fear.

"Now, I'll tell you one thing," the interrogator said, leaning forward again. "We're going to get the truth out of you sooner or later. Right now Colonel Correy's being a real wuss about prisoners, so you've got it easy. But if you swampers pull any more tricks out of your grubby little sleeves, he'll change his tune real quick." He smiled a cat-and-canary smile. "And then, you and me, we'll get to know each other *real* well, sweetheart."

"Lieutenant Commander Samuel Roberts Sloan, Guardians. Social Security number 585-36-2346," Sam said, his eyes fixed firmly on the bulkhead half a meter above Colonel Correy's battleship-gray flattop.

"You're a goddam traitor," growled the colonel.

"Sir, I can't help but notice you're wearing the insignia of the Federated States of Europe," said Sloan in his best Ozark hillbilly drawl. "Might I remind the colonel that, according to the Constitution, anyone who enters the service of a foreign prince relinquishes the rights of American citizenship?"

The colonel's open hand slammed down on his desk so hard all the pens and pencils leaped out of a holder made from a cut-down thirty-millimeter shell. "Don't hand me that, you bastard!" He was on his feet, shaking with fury. "This country was flat on its back, beneath a damned pussyfooting usurper President who wasn't doing one damned thing for her. The Federated States of Europe tried to lend a helping hand, restored the real President of the United States. And you"—he was standing in front of Sloan now, stabbing him in the sternum with a granite-hard finger—"you *assassinated* him!"

"President Lowell was a puppet, controlled by Chairman Maximov through W. Soames Summerill, also known as Trajan. William Lowell," he said, eyes still fixed above the colonel's head, "was a traitor to his country. Sir."

Correy slapped him.

Sloan's head rocked with the blow, then snapped back eyes-front. He never made a sound. Correy turned away.

"I'm sorry. That was unprofessional of me."

He returned to his seat. "Unless you're a deserter, it means the rest of the Guardians are on the ground here too. I can only think of one thing which might have brought you here, though how you found out about it, I don't know. That's one of the things it's going to be up to Political Officer Myers to discover. Mr. Charles, here"—he nodded at the stocky ex-attorney, who stood to one side looking like a bulldog to Myers's whippet—"has rendered his country a signal service. I'll see personally that he gets a medal for it."

Sloan smiled. "I think thirty pieces of silver's the more traditional reward."

Correy went white. Charles started forward, his face turning the color of an eggplant, shouting, "I'm not going to let any damned traitor who runs with stinking drug pushers talk to me like that!"

Myers took him by the arm as Captain Mancuso hastily interposed himself between the furious man and Sloan. "Take it easy, now, John. You know you did the right thing."

Some of the color had returned to Correy's craggy face. "So you've added blasphemy to your list of other accomplishments, Commander." He folded his hands before him, with obvious effort, as if arthritis had stiffened the joints. "Very well. Political Officer, take him away. For the first time in my career, I find myself in the presence of someone who fully deserves your boys."

The fist collided with Sloan's cheek like the kick of a mule. He blinked several times, lolled his head forward again, feeling his teeth with his tongue. He tasted blood, but nothing seemed broken. "You're going to bust your hand doing that, son," he said to the athletic-looking young man in the gray and indigo of the FSE Special Police, who resembled a young Steve McQueen. The kid massaged his fist and glared at him.

He was bound to a chair in what was probably a crew cabin, with a little head in the back and a couple of bunks folded up into the wall. Sheets of eight-mil plastic had been laid meticulously over the carpet and dogged down with duct tape. The plastic also lined the bulkheads to about chest level.

"You run a very neat torture chamber here, Myers," Sloan said to the political officer, who sat in a folding auditorium chair to one side with his elbows propped on his knees. He wore civilian clothes, tan trousers and a white shirt.

"Why, thanks, Commander," he said. "By the way, if you like, you can call me Seneca. I was with the Roman faction of the Company, too, just like my late lamented colleague Trajan. I believe you were acquainted?"

"I had the misfortune." Another punch caught him. "Whoo. Blindsided me there, son. Think that one gave me whiplash; practically turned my head so I could look over my shoulder like an old hoot owl." He looked back at Myers. "You're really aren't going to get anything out of me like this, you know."

Myers grinned. "Of course not, Commander. Your friend Mr. Charles told us everything we needed to know. This is just for recreation."

Somewhere a bullfrog made his basso puking sounds. Billy McKay stood by the creek with his big arms folded across his chest, smelling the night smells, letting the mosquitoes eat his face unmolested.

"I am sorry I ran away," Ron Bouchoux said in a husky voice. "I should have stayed, tried to help."

His left arm was wrapped in an old-fashioned sling that looked ghostly in the light of a quarter moon. A big 7.62 slug from one of the ambushers' rifles had caught him as he fled into the night. Fortunately it had passed cleanly through his upper arm without hitting the bone, traveling just a bit under the speed necessary to produce bad hydrostatic shock. He'd make a quick and complete recovery, unless of course some kind of hateful swampland infection caught him.

"Yeah, you're fucking-A straight," McKay said out of the side of his mouth. "You should have stayed right there and got your ass shot off, and then we wouldn't have had idea one we'd been compromised until the fucking Effsees started dropping out of the sky right on top of us."

"What he means, son," said Rogers softly, "is that you

did the right thing. Courage got nothing to do with throwing your life away uselessly."

The young man shook his head, dark eyes glistening with tears.

It was probably bad security to stay in Falcon house, but at least for tonight they were going to do it anyway. The hard time Jenny had given him this afternoon notwithstanding, the Effsees were not going to push a surface thrust this far without giving plenty of notice. And as for dropping out of the sky in helicopters—McKay almost smiled at the prospect. Achille Falcon had returned from delivering Casey Wilson back to Mobile One with his airboat *Minou Noir—Black Cat*—loaded with shoulder-fired antitank and antiaircraft missiles. Billy McKay would just *love* to give a chopperload of Effsee fuckers a taste of one of those Stingers.

"If you want to try to rescue Commander Sloan," Ron said, "please take me along."

McKay grimaced. He'd been tempted. It was just the sort of mission he'd reveled in, excelled in, when he had served with Studies and Observations Group, Southwest Asia Command, in the Med.

The bad guys would have Sam on board the liner they used for a troop ship—piece of cake. Nothing he hadn't done a dozen times, not much different from sneaking aboard that Dutch freighter in Abadan to lay aces of spades on the chests of sleeping crewmen, to give them a gentle hint of just what might happen if they continued to supply America's enemy Iran with armaments; or the "bol bean" mission in Tobruk harbor, substituting ammunition loaded with high explosives instead of propellant powder, that would blow a shooter's head off when he tried to fire it, for 7.62 Russian Short cartridges awaiting offloading in the hold of a Soviet ship. Just him and Rogers—fucking Effsees wouldn't have a chance.

He squeezed his eyes shut. There he was, doing it
again. Tom had already poured cold water on the scheme.
They had a job to do, and it wasn't rescuing Sam Sloan.
Until the mission was accomplished, they couldn't chance
having one of the Guardians still on the loose stop a stray
round, at least not on any wild-ass Errol Flynn attempts to
rescue their buddy. It was hard, but it was what being a
Guardian was all about. Sometimes McKay could almost
hate Rogers, for always being right.

Rogers clapped Bouchoux on the shoulder. "C'mon,
let's go have a couple of drinks and then turn in." Trans-
lated, that meant Rogers was going to ease enough booze
down the boy to get him unwound, then tuck him into bed.
Rogers had a gift for handling men that was at least as
great as his gift for dirty warfare. "Good night, Billy."

"'Night." He sensed Tom's eyes on him. "Just think I'll
stand out here a bit. You know, commune with nature, the
mosquitoes, that sort of shit."

They left him there. He stood watching the dead water
ease by with the stars dancing on it, the reflection of a
firefly weaving in and out among them like a meteorite
with a mind of its own. Around him the cicadas buzzed
rhythmically, the bull frogs boomed and the banjo frogs
gave their breathless trills.

Off to the left something splashed loudly. He stiffened,
hand going to the butt of his .45. "Don't be afraid," a voice
said behind him. "It's just a big snapper slipping into the
water. Didn't make near enough noise for an alligator—
not that you have to worry about them either. If you leave
them alone, they leave you alone."

He turned. It was Jenny Robidoux. She wore a sun-
dress, light with some kind of faint pattern on it, that
seemed to glow against her sun-darkened skin. "Sort of
like you folks, huh."

She laughed. "Sort of."

He gazed out over the bayou again. The firefly wandered off into the cypress. *"Mouche à feu,"* she said, falling in beside him. "I used to catch them when I was little, put them in a jar for a lantern. Then I would feed them to my anole—the little lizards they sell as chameleons in pet stores. I was a very bad little girl."

"Glad to see you turned out all right."

She stood there in silence for a while. He realized he was becoming very aware of her, and the scent of warm, healthy female flesh, smelling faintly still of soap. *Great. All I need is to get the hots for some broad who'd like nothing better than to cut my dick off and dry it out for a swizzle stick.*

"He is a friend of yours?"

He didn't need to ask who she was talking about. "Something like that. More than that, maybe. A buddy. Almost . . . almost like a brother."

She nodded. "I understand. I lost one brother in Nicaragua, before the war. And two sisters after, to typhus. I understand."

There was what seemed like a lot more silence. He flexed his shoulders, to try and let some of the tension out of them. "Well, I think I'll be getting back—"

She slipped her arm through his. "Why don't you come with me?"

"Where?"

"Somewhere private."

A trifle numb, he allowed himself to be led along the bank. "I always hated Sylvester Stallone," she remarked. "But when I was a little girl, I always had a crush on Jim McMahon, the football player. If you had more hair, you'd look just like him—only not as pretty, of course. But then, these days, beggars cannot be choosers, *non?*"

CHAPTER
THIRTEEN ──────────────

The bridge of the FSS *General Marshall* was dark except for the blue-and-red glow of instruments. An officer and a rating slouched in the gloom, eyes heavy with midwatch torpor. Around sunset a patrol had reported sighting the mysterious light in the sky, but it was long gone, and ceasing to be a source of excitement anyway: swamp-gas jokes were already making the rounds. Over on the *Newport* lights were showing, and clangs and curses drifted across the still water from time to time as the poor blighters over there made ready for the big push inland. The water around the LST was full of lighters and ground-effects craft moving toward shore. Lieutenant Cox did not half envy the bastards, having to muck about in that terrible swamp. He was no fool; he'd pick tedium over adventure any day.

"Sir." It took a moment for him to realize the rating had spoken.

"Yes, Barstow, what is it?"

"I've something on the radar, sir."

Grumpily, the lieutenant boosted himself off his seat. He was a wispily built young man with slightly protuberant eyes, who did not look the type to have served with distinction on the frigate HMS *Fearless*, during the furious North Atlantic battles that preceded the One-Day War, but he had. He came forward to peer over the rating's shoulder. There was a yellow blob onscreen.

"It's quite a sizable return, sir. It seems to be a ship, underway outside Cat Island Pass, about five miles past the Isles Dernieres." He gave the name a schoolboy-French pronunciation.

"So I see," Cox said.

"Hadn't we better pass the word for the captain, sir?" The rating looked up at him, the yellow glow of the scope underlighting his round face making him resemble Peter Lorre about to throw the switch in Frankenstein's castle.

"Why bother? It's just a squall." His service with the Royal Navy had made him very cautious about troubling his superiors unnecessarily.

"But sir, it looks very much like a frigate."

"And have you never seen a rain squall give a return that looked just like a frigate?"

"Well . . . yes, sir. Many times."

"You see, then? Carry on, Barstow. And we'll not trouble the captain unless this little rain squall of yours does something unsquall-like."

The bass thrumming of the engines died away to idle, turning the twin screws of the *Cienfuegos* only enough to keep headway. "We have target separation now, Comrade Captain," a technician reported from the console of the Head Net C radar. "Two large targets, bearing three-five-one, range, twenty-four thousand meters."

"The liner and the LST, just as our recon boat reported," Cardenas said.

Asusta nodded, smiled. "Excellent. The boat reported the liner lies to the west?"

"Aye, Comrade Captain."

"Very well. Commence programming sequence. We'll take the target to port first."

"Aye-aye, sir. Programming sequence commenced. Portside target."

"Poor bastards," the captain said, shaking his head. "They don't even know we're here."

"Apparently the . . . unidentified aircraft shot down their helicopter before it reported our presence," the exec said.

The corner of Asusta's mouth turned down in sardonic amusement. "To be rescued by a flying saucer sounds like a bourgeois science fantasy, doesn't it? A curious world we live in, these days."

"Program sequence completed, sir."

"Commence arming sequence."

"I wonder what the imperialists are doing here," Cardenas said, peering out into the blackness. Even at this distance, he could see the lights twinkling inshore.

"Who knows? Maybe they're conducting maneuvers. Whatever they're doing, they're about to be interrupted."

"Missile armed and ready, sir."

Asusta stooped to pick up Neruda, who was standing over his shoe and vibrating, sensing his master's excitement. Cardenas didn't bother to mask his relief. It offended the executive officer's sense of propriety to have the beast underfoot, going into action.

"Time we paid the imperialists back for what they did to our island," Asusta said. "Fire."

"Sir!" Barstow's voice hit a high note. "I'm picking up another return—something small, moving quite fast—"

But Cox, standing with his hands behind his back gazing out to sea, had seen the distant flash. He knew instantly what it was. Since Tuesday, May 4, 1982, every British Naval man had known one overriding dread. What rode that little blue-white spark of light—like a star on the horizon, actinic, almost too bright to look at, hardly seeming to move—was, simply, death.

The light winked out. Cox was not deluded; he knew the booster burn lasted mere seconds. "Sound the alarm, Barstow," he said calmly. "Then I suggest you place your arms over your face."

Barstow punched a button. The raucous wail of klaxons filled the ship. Then he did as he was told—he was Royal Navy, too.

"For what we are about to receive," he heard the lieutenant say, over the ululation of the horns, "dear Lord, make us thankful."

Gabriel's trumpet, sounding a little flat, wasn't enough to rouse a semicomatose Sloan. The Crack of Doom itself was another matter. It punched him out of the bunk and sent him skidding across the deck like a hockey puck.

His entrails knew what had happened long before his mind was even fully conscious. After all, he had a much more immediate experience of shipkilling missiles than even the Royal Navy boys who mostly crewed this barge.

Blearily he started to get to his feet. His entire body hurt like hell, and his face felt as if it had been used to hammer nails. *Those bastards really worked me over well*. He drew some satisfaction from the fact that some of his playmates of the afternoon were not going to make it through this.

Of course, neither was he. He let himself lie back down. Getting up was too much effort for somebody who was going to die. Already it seemed the vessel had begun to tilt to starboard and settle by the bows. She was either going to sink or burn to the waterline, that much was certain. Lightly built as she was, HMS *Sheffield* had been a warship, meant to absorb at least a certain amount of damage, and one punch from an Exocet had sent her to the bottom.

It was a good bet Sloan would be entombed in this little locked cabin, far aft on the lower deck. He might last for several days until his air ran out—unless the vessel burned before it sank, in which case fire would get him first. He wasn't sure how much of an improvement that would be. It was a hell of a note on which to end his distinguished career as a naval hero and Guardian.

Guardian. That exclusive fraternity was about to be reduced by twenty-five percent. But as long as he belonged to it, he was at least going to die standing up. With a convulsion of his stomach muscles he brought his upper body upright. His head whirled like a tumbled gyro. *Well, sitting up, anyway,* he amended mentally.

Outside the hatch there was a great deal of confusion, running feet, shouting voices, screaming. He even imagined he could hear the rush of flames. He could definitely feel the gurgle of inrushing water. The Cubans were to be congratulated; they'd scored a waterline hit on the *Marshall*. That settled one question: Unless this liner was a lot more inflammable than he thought it was, he was safe from fire, because the ship was definitely going down in a hurry.

Another explosion. Sam winced. He might be among enemies, but the sounds of a ship in agony affected him the same way as did the screaming of a dog hit by a car.

He realized that this explosion hadn't jarred loose whatever teeth the sons of bitches might have left him, the way it would have had the Cubans for some reason felt the need for a follow-up strike on the *Marshall*. He guessed at once that the Cubans had instead directed their next strike at the big boxy LST. Sloan grinned. Empathy for dying ships was one thing, but this was going to put one hell of a cramp in the Effsee plans concerning Project Starshine.

On the other hand, most of their troops and a good portion of their heavy equipment were already ashore. That was too bad. He'd rest a lot easier if he thought Maximov's plans might die with him.

By sheer willpower he forced himself to his feet. He stood there braced with both hands on the bulkhead, realizing that he wasn't going to have to worry about burning or suffocation, either one, because his head was shortly going to just fall apart.

The door opened. A beautiful woman in a T-shirt and jeans with black hair hanging past her shoulders stood there silhouetted by lights in the corridor.

"Oh," Sloan said. "I've started hallucinating. At least my last hours won't be boring."

The woman frowned at him, gave her head a little shake as if trying to clear water from her ears. Smoke was seeping into the room, water slopping over the sill.

"Are you a Guardian?" the apparition asked.

"Yes, ma'am. And I have to congratulate my subconscious for coming up with a fantasy that looks like you."

"I'm June-Marie Landry." She stepped up to him, thumbed up his eyelids in turn. "You don't *seem* to be concussed."

"I'm not?"

"You're sure talking like you are. Come on. We have to warn them at Wolf Bayou."

"Say what?"

"Project Starshine! Isn't that why you're here?" She grabbed his wrist. "We have to *go*."

"Does everybody know about this but me?" Sam demanded as she hauled him out into the passageway.

"Some soldier let me out of the room I was locked in," she explained, in answer to a question Sam hadn't asked.

"They're letting all the prisoners out. Except you, I guess."

The passageway was filled with smoke from chest level up, dense and dark and choking. The deck was three centimeters deep in water. Far forward Sam could see water welling into the passage as though from a spring, a lot of people milling about, flames and smoke.

"I guess we head aft," he said.

WHAM! A round cracked past his head as he turned. Somebody screamed as it found a target. Sam ducked back against the bulkhead as June-Marie threw herself to the other side of the passage.

Young Steve McQueen was standing there with one sleeve of his uniform jacket burned half off and a pistol in his hand. "Making a break for it, you son of a bitch? Well, I think I can stop that—"

He aimed the pistol lower. June-Marie reached behind her, grabbed a little red fire extinguisher out of its brackets on the bulkhead, and hurled it at him. Young McQueen pivoted, fired a shot that scarred paint an inch from her ear, reflexively batted at the fire extinguisher with his gun hand.

Sloan took two skipping sideways steps toward him, lashed out with a sort of straight-legged sidekick for which Major Moon, their Korean karate instructor, would smilingly have kicked his ass around the mat six or seven times for. It worked just fine. The side of his boot caught the man's hand, sent the pistol spinning away.

Sloan planted his right foot, snapped a spinning backkick with his left into the pit of the Effsee's belly. The man gasped and doubled over. Sloan side-kicked him in the face, nailed him in the gut again as the force of the blow straightened him out.

As the man jackknifed a second time he squared and fired a front snap kick so savage he was way off-balance when the ball of his foot caught the man in his jaw. There was a crack like a pistol shot. Steve McQueen, Jr., went down in a sprawl. His head lolled way over at a funny angle on his neck, and his eyes sort of stared up at the overhead flickering fluorescents.

Sloan stood above him, hands balled into fists, chest heaving like a winded racehorse. *I've just beaten a man to death,* he thought blankly. *How odd.*

"Take off your coveralls," June-Marie told him.

He blinked stupidly at her. "Somebody might recognize your uniform coveralls. But there are about two hundred guys in shirts and shorts up top. You'll blend right in."

He nodded, kicked off his boots and as quickly as his tortured limbs would allow skinned out of his camouflage coveralls. He wondered just who the hell this extremely competent young woman might happen to be.

She scooped up the pistol, tossed it to him. It was an H&K P9, successor to the Browning Hi-Power as the hip handgun. He stared at it for a moment as if unsure what it was.

"Take this. I don't know how to use it."

He nodded spastically, stuck the gun down the front of his skivvies. The cool barrel poked at him in a most peculiar place. *I hope the safety doesn't slip off before I have to grab this thing,* he thought wildly. *That could really be what they call going off half-cocked.*

No one seemed to have noticed the little vignette, or if they had, they had better things to think about. The deck no longer ran with water, and was displaying a pronounced tilt forward and to starboard.

"We're going down," Sloan said. "They'll have an aft ladder on a passenger ship. We'll go that way."

They ran.

The cheering had finally stopped echoing around the darkened bridge of *Cienfuegos*. Asusta watched the two ships burn with an angry yellow light. "I don't think we have to worry any more about them interfering with us," he remarked. "Good shooting, comrades."

"We'd best be careful, Captain," Cardenas said. "We don't know whether they have antiship missile launchers ashore."

Asusta scratched Neruda behind his floppy left ear. "Hmm. A good point. No point tempting fate, is there? Helmsman, shape a course back to our anchorage."

Up top, boats had been swayed over the side and queues had formed for them along the after promenade deck. Everything was as orderly as a drill—at least at this end of the ship. Forward was a different story.

The Cuban frigate had made a beautiful shot. The missile had struck at an acute angle almost exactly abeam of the bridge, driving well forward and clear to the centerline before exploding. The blast had torn out the right side of the bow. The forward part of the ship was a mass of flames that seemed to dance as high as the bridge itself. It looked like a home movie from hell up there, screams and escaping steam and burning men leaping into the sea, survivors fighting like mad things for the boats.

The stern was coming slowly up out of the water with a continuous vast sucking sound, but there were no signs of panic. An odd, detached calm seemed to possess everybody. Sloan wondered if everyone would be so calm if they knew just how likely this ship was to turn turtle with a wound like that. Possibly they would; disaster had strange effects on people.

He glanced around, a little wildly, considered leaping the railing and making a swim for it. Without a word June-Marie took her place in line. Feeling fresh admiration for her cool, he joined her.

"If she starts to go, jump fast, as far as you can," he

whispered in her ear. She nodded. He put his arm around her, tentatively at first. She snuggled against him as if hungry for some human contact.

"This is Acting Captain Cox," the PA system crackled. "All hands, abandon ship. All hands, abandon ship." Nobody needed telling twice. The line moved forward briskly.

Sam and June-Marie were scrambling down a rope ladder into a waiting lifeboat when they heard a crackle as of machine-gun fire from the bow. Sloan froze.

"Secondary explosions," somebody said from the boat. "Munitions stowage." Hurriedly, they climbed down and dropped into the boat.

There were a score of people aboard, including six or seven badly burned men. As Sam took an oar and helped pull away from the stricken liner, June-Marie closed her eyes very tightly, shuddered briefly. Then she opened her eyes and began helping a man with a first-aid kit tend to the injured.

As he rowed, Sloan studied the LST. The afterdeck was a mass of flames but the fire-control parties seemed to be bringing them under control. To his experienced eye it was obvious that the LST, much tougher than *Marshall* to begin with, had been struck only a glancing blow. She might survive the night yet. His emotions on the subject were mixed.

Their boatmates buzzed with dazed speculation. "Who was it? Who hit us?"

"Must have been the Russians."

"Naw, it was that flying saucer."

"Bullshit. I heard there were Cubans over to Atchafalaya Bay. They were the ones—"

"I heard the Guardians were here."

"The Guardians."

"Yeah, those traitor bastards musta done this—"

Smearing white zinc oxide cream on blackened skin,

June-Marie caught Sam's eye. And winked.

They were halfway to the shore, and Sam's muscles were beginning to protest despite the adrenaline charge that had blasted through them, when he heard a huge gurgling-sucking from aft of the boat. "Pull like hell!" he shouted. "She's going over!"

There were a couple of nautical-looking types aboard, and the rest were soldiers, who didn't have a clue as to what he was talking about. But his urgency and a volley of fresh screams from the stricken ship got the message across. Everyone began to row for all he was worth.

Facing astern as the rowers were, they soon found out what the excitement was about. Looking for all the world like a model in a George Pal bathtub, the big white liner began to tip, slowly at first, then gathering momentum like a boulder rolling downhill. Men whose turn for the boats hadn't come slid yelling across her deck to pitch into the blood-warm water as the ship rolled over on them. With awful majesty, creaking and groaning, burbling like an enormous baby, the ship capsized.

Heads bobbed on the water between liner and lifeboat. Many of them disappeared, sucked under by the suction of the huge ship turning turtle. Despite the efforts of the rowers, it caught the lifeboat like a maelstrom, pulled it around broadside before they could get headway again.

Sloan looked back at the ship as they got their craft moving toward shore again. One man had somehow made it to the keel as *Marshall* rolled, sat there now just forward of the naked screws, king of a mountain of dripping hull. He looked lonely and somehow thoughtful, perched there, as the ship began to slide under by the bows. Sloan snapped him a salute, then put his back into rowing.

Among the reeds next to a cypress stand Sloan slumped on his oar in the stern of the little boat while June-Marie helped the wounded wade to more or less dry land. "No, no," he heard her saying. "You stay here, we'll take her back."

"We can't let you go back there," somebody protested. Sloan dropped a hand to the butt of the P9.

"We're going back, dammit, and that's that!"

"You can't go alone—"

"You've done enough," Sloan called. "We'll take it from here."

Before any more argument could arise, June-Marie waded back to the boat and climbed in. As they pulled away, Sloan heard somebody say, "I don't know who those two are, but I sure as hell wish I did. They deserve a medal."

June-Marie looked at him, and her eyes seemed to twinkle by the light of the burning LST. "Shall I tell them?"

He shook his head. "No. After all, we aren't really going to merit the citation."

CHAPTER
FOURTEEN ─────────────────

"Bayou Teche," June-Marie said, gesturing off west across the early-morning waters of Sixmile Lake. "It used to be built up, with houses all along its banks, sugar plantations, motels, gas stations—everything. Now—" She shook her head. "There's hardly anything left. Except a few of the big old houses, that already survived a century of storms. Sometimes I don't think man *matters,* Sam."

He patted her hand. This morning she seemed very different from the cool, competent woman who had helped him escape certain death on the *Marshall* three days before. There seemed to be several people living beneath that smooth olive skin, and he was never sure which one he was going to meet.

"I know what you mean."

Behind them Ron Bouchoux loafed at the tiller, wearing nothing but Bermuda shorts, a battered Panama hat, and

mirror shades. He looked like a drug dealer off some
glossy eighties TV series. Behind him the lazy vee of their
wake intersected that of Jenny Robidoux's boat, thirty
meters ahead and offset a bit to port. They might have been
out for a day's fishing, or bound on a camping expedition
up some quiet bayou. Instead they were headed for mysterious Wolf Bayou—and Project Starshine.

Up in the boat ahead Casey Wilson, looking quite ca-
sual and comfortable in his Rush tour cap and inevitable
yellow Zeiss shooting glasses, was talking animatedly with
Jenny, while Billy McKay lay flaked out with his boonie
hat over his eyes. Tom Rogers was holding the fort by
himself back at the Cayen house, a few kilometers away
from the compromised Falcon headquarters, organizing the
resistance and keeping tabs on his buddies via the big
scrambler-equipped radio Casey had brought back from his
flying trip in Mobile One to a cache northeast of Vicksburg
in Mississippi.

Casey's main cargo that run had been all the shoulder-
fired antitank and antiaircraft missiles he could load into
the big V-450 armored car. That wasn't all. Though he had
been on his way back from the cache better than half a day
before Frank Hardisty had found Sloan and June-Marie
pulling for Bayou Grand Caillou eight or nine klicks northwest of Cocodrie, he had taken it upon himself to bring
along a virtually full replacement kit for Sam Sloan, including new cammie coveralls, web gear, and Galil/M-203
combination rifle and grenade launcher.

"I didn't think, like, it was your karma to die just now,"
the boyish former fighter pilot had explained with a perfectly straight face, shaking Sam's hand on his own return.
And even Sam Sloan, who sometimes to his distress was a
lot closer to being on Casey Wilson's out-of-the-way wave-
length than the other two Guardians, had no idea if this
paradoxical California kid was joking. You could never tell

with Casey. He was sort of a mixture of Chuck Norris and Lawrence Ferlinghetti.

For half a day they cruised northwest along Sixmile Lake, which as a bored Billy McKay irritably pointed out, was a damned sight longer than six miles. It was a clear day, lazy and hot. Eventually they swung north into a broad bayou, which June-Marie identified as a channel of the Atchafalaya River.

At about three o'clock they stopped off to stretch their legs at a relatively clear stretch of bank, next to a grove of green ash trees. They didn't hang around a long time. Despite the blow the Cubans had given them, the Effsees were a long way from out of it.

According to the latest word up the bayous, Colonel Correy and most of his staff, along with PO Myers, had survived the disaster. Former Assistant U.S. Attorney John Charles, the story said, was still in the *General Marshall*, which rested on the bottom of Terrebonne Bay with just the tip of her stern protruding above the water. Nobody seemed terribly grieved by that, least of all Sam Sloan. But the Effsees had somehow worked out where Starshine was located, and could be counted on to keep trying for it.

Which was why June-Marie Landry was leading the Guardians there. Just how the hell she knew about it, none of them had a clue. Under the circumstances, all they could do was trust her.

The bayou wound round and about between densely wooded banks. Here and there they passed vast mats of vegetation, alive with pale purple flowers of startling beauty. "Water hyacinth," June-Marie explained. "Back before the war they were a major pest. They'd take over the waterways if they weren't held back with chemicals. But now—" She shrugged. "For some reason they're nowhere near so aggressive. It's like the war turned everything upside down."

They proceeded, making apparently random turns into side channels at irregular intervals. As the sun started down and darkness began to gather, they turned east up an insignificant little creek whose opening no one would have noticed had June-Marie not pointed it out to them. After several hundred meters it took a turn northward and suddenly opened out into a marshy stretch a couple of hundred meters wide, bordered by the omnipresent cypress woods.

A nutria passed them, swimming the other way, his stubby muzzle in the air, ignoring them. Here the water was carpeted with a green down of duckweed that closed around the boats as they slowed.

"Wolf Bayou," June-Marie said, as they drifted a moment with engines on idle.

"Spooky," Casey observed, more with relish than trepidation.

"I don't see a damned thing," McKay said across the five meters of water that separated the two tiny boats. "Are you sure this is the right place?"

June-Marie nodded. "Fuck it," McKay grunted, "and drive on."

"You don't talk that way in front of a lady," Jenny corrected sharply.

"Damned straight. Let's go."

They hadn't gone a hundred meters before Jenny let out a yell and almost released the tiller. Even Casey Wilson sat up straight.

From the woods to their left a light arose, big and egg-shaped, glowing yellow like a misshapen moon. It drifted over to hover directly in their path, hung there a moment, not a hundred meters ahead, seeming to regard them.

"*Sacré Coeur*," breathed Ron. The light moved forward.

McKay had his M-60 in his hands on the off chance he

might be able to do anything with it. Sam Sloan didn't even bother to pick up his Galil. He'd seen what the UFO could do, even though the others could not quite bring themselves to believe the story he and Ron had told of what they saw in Atchafalaya Bay.

Only June-Marie appeared unmoved.

A spotlight stabbed down from the UFO, pinning them. Casey Wilson softly whistled the five-note theme from *Close Encounters of the Third Kind* between his teeth, and despite the tension Sloan had to laugh.

As the craft approached, they became aware of a muted humming sound. At the same time the object lost its amorphous quality, began to resolve itself into a shape—a winged craft the size of a small airplane, with propeller engines mounted in streamlined cowlings at the wingtips. At the moment the engines were tipped almost straight up, the multibladed propellers whirling horizontally like miniature helicopter rotors. The whole thing was cloaked in what looked for the world like mirrored Mylar and fitted with an array of lights arranged to break up its outline in a diffuse glow.

"Jesus *Christ*," Billy McKay said in disgust, "it's a fucking verti." At this range it unmistakably was one of the half-airplane, half-helicopter craft that over the last several years had assumed a number of tasks previously carried out by military helicopters.

Sloan's eyes were fixed on a glass-fronted sponson that bulged along the portside of the fuselage from the cockpit aft. "Billy," he said softly, "I'm damned if I don't think that thing mounts a laser. A big one."

"Yeah. And it's pointing this way. So what are we going to do about it?"

Moving with exaggerated caution, so as not to upset the narrow boat, June-Marie got to her feet and waved. Then she eased herself back down. "I sure hope she knows what she's doing," Ron said to no one in particular.

The muffled engines got a fraction louder. True to its name, the verti rose straight up, pivoted, moved off to the north. Sloan was amazed at how quickly it lost definition, transformed itself again into an amorphous UFO.

"We can go on now," June-Marie said quietly.

They followed the craft. Before long they came to a line of trees that marked the edge of what looked to be a couple of acres of solid ground. They skirted the island until they came to a pier that rested on cement pilings. They made the boat fast and stepped ashore.

"Doesn't look like much," McKay said, pulling out a cigar. In the middle of the bare island stood a couple of buildings that resembled Quonset huts, several cement blockhouses, and a squat, fifteen-meter-tall structure that looked like a very fat grain silo. The place looked pretty thoroughly abandoned.

June-Marie led them forward. As they approached the buildings, the verti settled toward a concrete apron lying on a bed of the inevitable crushed clamshells. The whisper of its engine subsided to silence, the multibladed propellers flickered into visibility. A hatch opened at the side of the cockpit and a man stepped out.

He was tall and rangy, with a beak nose and flamboyant mustache. By the glow of his aircraft the Guardians could see his dark hair was graying at the temples, though he appeared to be in his mid-thirties. His right hand was an aluminum hook.

June-Marie ran to him. He caught her in his arms and spun her around. He was a good deal taller than she. *"Jeune-Marie! Ma 'tite!"*

"Luc." She stood on tiptoe to kiss his cheek. "Luc, these men are the Guardians. They are here to find Project Starshine."

Eyes narrowed, Luc scanned the faces of the Guardians.

He came toward Casey Wilson, who had folded his glasses and tucked them in a pocket as a minor concession to the fact that it was damned near pitch-dark. A smile split his swarthy face.

"You're Wilson? First Lieutenant Kenneth C. Wilson, USAF?"

"Yo," said Casey, "that's me."

The big man ran forward with such suddenness that McKay started to bring up his machine gun. Luc clapped Casey on the arm with his good hand, then stuck it out to shake his. "I'm Luc Landry—captain, U.S. Army. I've wanted to meet you for years!"

Casey did a take. "Not Werewolf One?" he asked.

"The same."

He grabbed Landry's hand in both of his and pumped away as if this were *his* long-lost brother, and not June-Marie's. McKay looked at Sloan with his forehead all rumpled up.

"Don't look at me," Sloan said. "Nobody tells me anything either."

Casey turned back to his buddies. "Don't you fellows know? This is *Loup-Garou* Landry, the best chopper jock in the U.S. Army!"

"Aw, shit," McKay said. "The tank buster?"

"That's me," the tall man affirmed. "Meeting the best fighter pilot of the generation. A historic moment, *non?*"

"During the Second World War," Dr. Jonas Calhoun explained, as he led the party down a set of cement stairs that seemed to lead into the center of the earth, "there was considerable fear of invasion or attack by the Germans along the whole Eastern seaboard and the Gulf Coast. This installation was originally built as an ammunition dump, against a possible strike against the Mississippi Delta. Apparently, it was also intended as a possible fall-back strongpoint in case the invasion went well. This complex is actually quite huge, gentlemen, cofferdammed to a depth of better than twenty meters, completely sealed in cement like a giant box. When we took it over in the years before the war, we had to do very little that would give external evidence of our presence. Except build our cooling tower, of course."

They came to a landing. Calhoun produced a card from a pocket of his lab coat, slid it into a slot next to a metal door. He was a short man, firmly settled in his fifties, with a big bald head fringed in curly white hair, wire-rim glasses perched on a fleshy nose, surprisingly bright blue eyes. Beneath his lab smock he wore a white shirt, narrow black tie, pressed slacks. He appeared to deserve the nickname "Kettle Belly," but despite his urgings none of the Guardians could bring themselves to call him by it.

"Cooling tower?" Sloan asked.

"Of course. Among other amenities, we possess what is almost certainly the world's most compact nuclear power plant. The tower is disguised as a feed silo for the various endangered species we're supposed to be preserving here."

The Guardians exchanged glances. They were having trouble reading this Dr. Calhoun. Once Luc Landry had brought them into the underground installation a party of plant-security types in blue jumpsuits had escorted them to Calhoun's office. He had greeted them with a cold, appraising stare out from beneath his bushy grizzled eyebrows, then got up and gone out without a word. Several minutes later he was back. "Well, gentlemen," he'd said, "I suppose it can do no harm to show you around. You should have some idea of what's at stake here before we discuss matters."

What's to discuss? McKay had been about to ask. A warning glance from Sloan stopped him. There was something funny going on here. It would be better to let the scientist explain just what at his own pace, without crowding him.

The door slid open. They stepped out onto a catwalk six or seven meters above a concrete floor. The room seemed to be thirty meters across and at least sixty long, crisscrossed with catwalks at various levels, crowded with machinery. A huge doughnut shape dominated the center of the brightly lit chamber. Technicians swarmed everywhere like termites in pastel coveralls and white lab coats.

Dr. Calhoun stopped and made an expansive gesture. "There it is, gentlemen—ladies. The future of America. Perhaps of the entire world: Apollo."

McKay frowned. "Apollo?"

"The world's first true fusion power generator."

A few minutes later they were back in Kettle Belly Calhoun's office in the uppermost subterranean floor. It was not a very big office to begin with, and was distinctly crowded by a desk with built-in computer, Kettle Belly and his belly, Luc Landry and his sister, and three Guardians. Ron and Jenny, awestruck by the whole thing, had been left in an antechamber under the discreet eye of a security man.

"Just to make it official, Doctor," McKay said, leaning back against an undressed cement wall, "we've come for the blueprints."

Calhoun folded his hands across his famous belly and frowned like a gnome. "I have to confess I expected to hear those words some time ago. It's been a long time since the war, gentlemen."

McKay scowled. "We been occupied."

The door opened and a young man came in pushing a wheeled tray with a coffeepot and cups. As he served, Sloan said, "If you could explain to us a little further about this setup you have here, Dr. Calhoun—"

"Call me Kettle Belly, please. It helps put me at ease." He accepted a cup of decaffeinated coffee. "It's really quite simple. Before the war we moved in here using the cover of the Wolf Bayou Wildlife Reclamation Center. We are in the middle of a federal wilderness area declared shortly before construction began; with public access to the area restricted—and the public has never exactly flocked to the heart of the Atchafalaya Basin to begin with—it was easier than you might expect to bring in the necessary materials, from various directions, over a period of months. Particularly inasmuch as the basic physical plant, as it were, was ready and waiting for us. All we had to do was clean it out and move in."

McKay knocked back a slug of coffee. "But how come everybody talks about Wolf Bayou like it's filled with monsters or something? And what is all this flying saucer jive?"

Calhoun sipped and nodded judiciously. "As you perceive, Lieutenant McKay, there is a connection. Even before the war it was in our interests to preserve the secrecy of our facility every way we could. We began spreading a few rumors here and there, that Wolf Bayou was not the healthiest place to be. After the war, the plague alleviated our problem for a time, but when people began to move back into the area, we could no longer rely on being in the middle of a wilderness zone to maintain our isolation; people tended to disregard such niceties amid the ruin of civilization. So we modified our aircraft, a McDonnell Douglas VX-20—it's a prototype, which had not entered production by the time of the war—modified it in such a way as to add a certain credence to the mystery of Wolf Bayou."

"I'd say installing a laser weapon's a pretty substantial modification, Doc—Kettle Belly," Sam Sloan said.

"Yeah. I ain't heard of no weapons like that being deployed," McKay said.

The physicist chuckled. "There are some very similar ones which were supposed to go into service before the war, though of course that wasn't common knowledge, even at your security clearance. But to produce laser-generated fusion, we required state-of-the-art lasers here, and have made substantial advances in the technology on our own. What I gather Commander Sloan witnessed in Atchafalaya Bay was a chemical laser in action. It's powered by prepacked cartridges. They're quite unwieldy; the normal load is four, each good for a single shot. Of course"—here he sipped his coffee—"we've never needed more than one at a time. People don't seem inclined to argue with a death ray from a flying saucer."

"What about blowing up that regulator truck?" McKay asked.

Calhoun shot a sour glance at Landry. "Our esteemed captain, here, from time to time finds himself unable to resist the temptation to play Sir Galahad."

Landry looked sheepish. "I figured they needed a lesson."

"Like, Captain, how did you wind up here, anyway?" Casey asked.

"I requested him. Though we've stockpiled supplies of all sorts sufficient to last us for several years—the only reason we were able to survive your dilatoriousness in contacting us—we found it necessary to bring in additional instruments from time to time, without benefit of roads. The VX-20 was ideal for our needs, and to pilot it, I thought we should have the best—the best rotary-wing pilot, that is," he finished with a nod to Casey.

Casey nodded back, smiling. "Also, I was a gunship pilot during the Vietnam conflict. Captain Landry here distinguished himself in just such a role, destroying some thirty tanks in the war on the Egyptian-Libyan frontier—"

"And a Frogfoot," interjected Casey.

"—as well as becoming the first American helicopter pilot to down a jet aircraft. I confess a certain amount of nostalgia went into my requesting the assignment of Captain Landry. And a certain vanity: as I said, I wanted only the best."

He glanced at June-Marie, shaggy brows lowering. "Finally, the captain's sister was employed on the project as a technician. I thought it would be a nice gesture to reunite them. Unfortunately, my thoughtfulness was insufficient to secure Ms. Landry's loyalty."

June-Marie's eyes blazed. Half-consciously Sam moved closer to her.

"How did you know about the regulators?" asked Casey. He sipped his drink. It was tea, of course, and not just any tea, but Celestial Seasonings Red Zinger. Casey was that way.

Landry shrugged. "Since the war we've periodically dropped off people on the outside, just to keep touch with events in our vicinity," Calhoun said. "We are not *totally* isolated from the rest of the world—as certain of our personnel claimed to believe we were."

He said this looking straight at June-Marie. She flushed angrily. "I couldn't take it any more, this living in a giant cement box, as if we were in a different world. And the way you sent my brother out to terrorize the people who lived around us, when we could have helped them so much during the desperate times!"

Kettle Belly turned pink clear to the top of his shiny, defoliated skull. "We had a lifeboat situation here, Ms. Landry," he rasped, his deep voice seeming to break up into fragments under stress. "What we are doing here, we are doing for the entire human race. We couldn't let false humanitarian concerns interfere."

That dropped the conversation in its tracks. For a few moments there was no sound but the clinking of china on china, and the rattle of a spoon as McKay, who had jolted himself awake with a cup of black coffee, decided to take some nourishment by half filling his second cup with sugar.

"Maybe we'd better talk about how we're going to get you back online with the Blueprint, Doctor," he said.

Kettle Belly leaned back in his chair and frowned. "That presents something of a problem, Lieutenant McKay."

McKay scowled. "Why do you say that, sir?" Sloan interposed hurriedly.

"Because I'm not at all sure that it is appropriate for us to do so."

Everyone stared at him hard enough to burn their eyes, except for Landry and his sister, who didn't seem to want to look at the doctor at all. "Mister, I think you got some explaining to do," McKay said.

Landry scowled at him, pulling his chair back a few degrees to face him squarely. McKay looked at him. The chopper pilot had an inch on him, but he had a good twenty pounds on his side, plus all his hands. He figured he could take him.

"Given that you were placed in charge of this vital facility as a component of Project Blueprint," said Sam, all ice-blue Commander Annapolis now, "it seems that Lieutenant McKay has asked an entirely appropriate question, Doctor."

Calhoun sighed. "That's true, Commander. But I'm afraid your legal standing is, ah, somewhat equivocal."

"What the hell is that supposed to mean?" McKay barked.

"Substantial question exists as to just who constitutes the rightful government of the United States."

"Jeff MacGregor's President," Casey said.

Calhoun raised brows like bleached caterpillars. "Is he? We have, I believe, a party of men from the Federated

States of Europe anchored in Terrebonne Bay, who likewise claim to represent the rightful government of the United States. Given your own—shall we say questionable—role in the deposition of President William Lowell, it is not at all apparent whose claim has legal force."

"You'd sell out to a bunch of fucking Effsees?" barked McKay.

Landry started to his feet. His sister stopped him with a hand on his flesh arm.

"Not sell out, Lieutenant," said Calhoun. "It is of supreme importance that stewardship over the power we have unleashed here pass into the proper hands. And I'm in the hot seat as far as figuring out who those proper hands belong to."

"That's fair enough," Sam said, though the words tried to stick in his throat. Trusting Casey to keep an eye on McKay so that he wouldn't start hitting people unless it became absolutely necessary, he sketched a story of the taking of Heartland by FSE shock troops and its aftermath. At the end of his narrative, Calhoun nodded.

"I must say, Commander, you've given me much food for thought. But even if I stipulate that you are telling the truth"—at this McKay made a noise like Godzilla first spying Tokyo across the bay—"then my course of action is still far from clear. Even if Jeffrey MacGregor is the rightful President of the United States of America, I have to ask myself: Is he truly the man to be entrusted with this power?"

McKay gripped the arms of his chair so tightly the hollow metal frame began to buckle. He, Sam, and Casey were hardly in a position to seize the facility themselves— at least at this point. "Well, *Doctor,* you just sit here and think about this moral dilemma of yours. And we'll go off for a while and kick Effsee butt, and when we're done with that, we'll come back and you can let us know what you worked out."

Calhoun's eyes skittered away from McKay's behind the thick lenses of his wire-rims. "I'm afraid it would be inadvisable for you to leave at this point."

"We have to get back, man," Casey protested. "The Effsees are going to move out any time."

"Precisely the problem, gentlemen. Until I decide which course is best, I just don't see how I can permit you to carry out attacks against soldiers of the FSE. American soldiers, might I add?"

"American traitors," McKay said.

"Not traitors, Lieutenant McKay," June-Marie said. "Only wrong."

Calhoun stood up. "There are ample rooms here to accommodate you, gentlemen. I will contact the commander of the Federated States expedition, get his side of the story, and after evaluating that—"

McKay scraped back his chair on the bare cement floor and stood. "We're going."

Calhoun frowned. "I thought I made it clear that you could not leave."

"Try and stop us."

"Sheer bravado," sniffed Calhoun. "I have a substantial security force on call. And if you're thinking of taking me hostage, let me advise you: don't. I've given orders to cover that contingency. The results would be unpleasant for us all."

"Shit, Doc, we don't have to mess with that. Did you forget that there are *four* Guardians? By now Tommy Rogers is out there in the swamp, all set up and waiting to hear from us. Just what do you think an eighty-two-millimeter round would do, dropped on top of that cooling-tower silo of yours?"

Calhoun paled. "You're bluffing! Your communicators can't possibly reach outside, not with all the steel reinforcing the concrete over our heads."

"That don't make no difference. If we don't walk out here free and clear by a certain time, Rogers starts shooting."

"You're lying!"

McKay gave him a good look at his incisors. "Try me."

Calhoun looked meaningfully at Landry. "If you must shoot at them, Luc," his sister said, "you must shoot at me also."

Calhoun drew a deep breath, held it, let it out. "I don't want to run afoul of any family loyalties here," he said in resignation. "And I can't afford any risk, however small, to the facility. You gentlemen may go.

"But I find it hard to envision myself entrusting the secret of fusion power to the likes of you!"

CHAPTER
FIFTEEN

"Some of the oldtimers think a storm is coming up, Billy," Tom Rogers said, hunkered down on a bank beneath a tupelo gum. "Could be a big one." McKay stood out in the open squinting up into the sky. The sun had barely come up, and it was well hidden by an overcast that blanketed the sky.

"Look at the haze," said Jenny Robidoux, sitting in her airboat, *Chouette*, nearby. The name meant either "sweetheart" or "classy," depending on how you chose to look at it. "When it hangs like that, it means there's weather coming."

McKay squinted north along the bayou where the trees closed in around it. There were patches of dense mist hanging like bits of ectoplasm a meter or so off the surface of the water. It looked too eerie to be real, somehow, but he said, "Now, that's what I call woodsy lore. Anybody could look at the sky and *see* there's weather coming."

Jenny sniffed.

They were on a spit of forested ground several kilometers west of Cocodrie. The several kilometers that separated them from the FSE beachhead consisted almost entirely of marsh, cut by clear channels and dotted with lakes and "mixing-bowl" ponds where sea water and fresh commingled. Here was where the Guardians hoped to strike the most concentrated blow at the Effsees as they began their hundred-kilometer trek to Wolf Bayou.

A score of airboats bobbed around the pool where the bayou emptied into the marsh, most of them painted with colorful names: *La Catin,* the doll; *Go to Hell;* a pair of boats from over to the Teche, *Acadian Driftwood* and *Gypsy Tailwind.* Next to Jenny's boat floated one painted with the curious name of *Shfal Job.* Somebody had explained to McKay that that was the English spelling of the Acadian way of pronouncing the bayou-dwellers' name for praying mantis: *cheval du diable,* or devil-horse. McKay was not sure he followed that.

The boat belonged to Black Jacques Weygand, a barrel-bodied bastard from Bayou LaFourche, in his early forties, with incredibly black hair, emphatic eyebrows and mustache, cheeks furred with a black half-centimeter growth, as if it was all of his beard any blade born could cut. He was, like McKay, a veteran of the Marines' Force RECON, which meant McKay was glad to see him no matter what he called his goddamned boat.

"Whoo-ee," said the incredibly skinny black kid in his early twenties who stood nearby. His name was Theron McDonald, and he was the nephew of old Whitey of the former Fina station. "We got every coonass, nigger, redbone, and white trash for miles around. How can we lose?"

McKay grinned. It remained to be seen how the kid

acted when the bullets started cracking past his ears like ripping canvas, and the shells going off around him and each one sounding like the end of the world its own self, but McKay liked to hear that sound of spirit.

"Radio check, McKay," Sloan's voice said in his ear. With Rogers and a bunch more airboats he was on another hummock a kilometer to the southwest.

The airboats were only a part of the overall scheme, if the flashiest. In all, several hundred men—and not a few women—were stretched out in little clumps in a crescent across the Effsees' line of advance, in boats or afoot even. The marsh was shallow, for the most part, and a man could wade it—if he knew where to put his feet. Otherwise he might unexpectedly find a hole, and that would be too bad.

"I read you loud and clear, Sam," McKay said. "Our radios work just fine, out here in the open. It's when we're up the creek that they glitch on us."

Sloan chuckled. "Care to rephrase that, over?"

Another voice said, "Blackbird, this is Cottonmouth, do you read, over?"

"Cottonmouth, this is Blackbird," Tom Rogers responded. He was sitting out the battle, directing operations over the big radio Casey had brought back from the cache. He had been chosen as controller because he had the best rapport with the locals. That suited McKay fine; it meant he got to kick some asses.

"Cottonmouth, this is Blackbird. I read you, over."

"They're moving."

A cheer met Casey's passing the word along. Mckay smiled crookedly. *We'll see*.

"Let's ride," he yelled.

"No question of this being a feint, Billy," Casey Wilson said over the communicators. He was two hundred meters away, but McKay wouldn't have been able to hear him had he been hunkered down at his elbow. The noise of ground-effects vehicles roared around them like a hurricane, overwhelming all other sound.

Ahead of McKay stretched a couple hundred meters of predominantly open pool. At the far side the advance elements of the FSE force broke into view: three of the big blowers, grinning sharks' mouths painted on the leading edges of their skirts, with a gaggle of power boats trailing behind.

"Casey, you take the one on the left. I get the one in the middle. Black Jack"—he refused to struggle with the French pronunciation—"you get the one on the right. Have your people ready to boogie and try again later if we miss one. These mothers are serious shit."

"No kidding." The other ex-Marine was among the few who really had some idea just how much firepower the hovercraft carried.

"Well, pass the word: no heroes."

McKay finished prepping his throwaway Armbrust anti-tank rocket. Behind him, seventeen-year-old Achille Falcon, his driver, crouched in front of the big caged fan of his boat *Minou Noir*. He had one hand on the throttle and one hand holding the pistol grip of an M-16. It was an A2, and it was not a civilian model; apparently after the plague died back some of the more enterprising bayou folk had helped themselves to equipment from the desolated Houma airbase.

The Effsees were playing it cautious. Since the Guardians had got back from Wolf Bayou two days ago, they'd had the locals start firing up the FSE patrols. And more: a whole squad had been captured a klick or so up Crazy Woman Bayou, not far from where McKay and Casey and their team awaited the FSE advance. Correy was using the blowers like tanks, leading off his columns with them. It was an old Red Army doctrine which the Soviets had cribbed straight from the German *Blitzkrieg*. Against modern, missile-armed troops, it was a good way to lose vehicles—but it was practically stone guaranteed to overrun untrained yokels with small arms.

McKay grinned. As a matter of fact, they *had* some of your modern missiles—and if most of the people firing them could hardly be defined as "troops," some of them at least were Guardians.

He lifted the thick tube to his shoulder, flipped up the sight. The lead air-cushion vehicle looked close enough to hit with a hard spit.

"Rock and roll," McKay said, and squeezed the firing stud. The Armbrust whooshed out of the tube and went spinning like an arrow for its target. Not for the first time McKay was glad they'd chosen to use the West German missiles instead of, say, American LAWs. Unlike most antitank rockets, Armbrusts produced neither a flash nor a backblast to give the shooter's position away.

His shot hit the pilot house of the lead vehicle just aft of the turret. It produced an insignificant-looking flash. At about the same moment Casey's rocket hit the starboard side of the cabin of his target, which almost instantly blew up with a great big bang and a lot of orange flame. The third vehicle, on the right wing of the echelon, started to hunt around with its turret weapon, a twin twenty-millimeter, blazing away with well-disciplined short bursts. Then Black Jacques's rocket hit the base of the turret. The twenty mike-mike rounds began going off by themselves like strings of Chinese firecrackers.

McKay's target had fallen off and begun to drift around as if uncertain where to go. The cabin was now illuminated from inside by an ugly red hellglow. Troopies clutching coal-scuttle helmets to their heads were bailing off the back as Casey's target just went on producing even bigger and better explosions. *Must be a munitions carrier,* McKay thought.

He raised a fist, shook it once. "Three for three!" he screamed at the marsh.

An explosion came from the lead hovercraft. McKay picked his M-60 up out of Falcon's airboat, held it against his shoulder by fore and rear pistol grips. Standing thigh-deep in the muck, he braced himself as best he could and started ripping short bursts into the men scrambling out of the hovercraft. Since this wasn't the movies, there was no way he was going to do much damage shooting like that at this range. But at the familiar, angry roar of the big machine gun, soldiers began to spill in all directions out of the boats following the hovercraft.

That was the point of the exercise, to encourage the boys to take a little swim. McKay knew how much foot sloggers *loved* to go crawling around in swamps. Since there was no way a couple of hundred swampers were going to defeat a minimum three hundred trained effectives in the long haul, the strategy for today was to cripple as much as possible of Correy's big mobility and firepower, bust up his organization, and demoralize his men. With luck, they might deprive his thrust of a lot of steam before it ever reached the cypress swamps.

Some of the soldiers trying to dive for cover were falling now, taking hits. The bayou militia seeded through the marsh had opened up now, with deer rifles, M-16s, anything to hand.

The gas tank on McKay's hovercraft finally blew up. Shots were cracking past him. The fierce muzzleblast of his Maremont was blowing the marsh grass to bits and throwing up a big cloud of debris; the Effsees had him spotted. He hopped back in the boat.

"Let's book," he told Falcon.

The boy grinned, the motor snarled, and the boat fish-tailed around in a turn and took off as if it had afterburners.

In incredulous fury, Sam Sloan watched his Armbrust draw a braided line of smoke right over the cabin of the lead hovercraft. *I can't have buck fever, it just isn't possible*, he thought.

What made it worse was that the other two AT rockets fired by his team had missed too. Three irreplaceable Armbrusts shot to hell.

The three hovercraft sailed serenely forward, out across a broad open channel. The civilians in his group had only been provided enough rockets for the one volley. It was an idea of Rogers's, intended first to keep the locals from burning up the weapons at too great a rate, and also to encourage them to keep peeling back to the dumps established on the cypress shore. Usually the big problem with civilians versus trained troops was getting them to stand and fight; in this case, Rogers was more afraid they *would* try to fight it out. And the balance of firepower was just too much on the Effsees' side.

Sloan had another Armbrust in the boat behind him. Instead he opted for a more familiar weapon, grabbed up his rifle and grenade launcher and sighted a grenade with a combination armor-piercing and fragmentation head on the lead hovercraft. That was one fortunate thing about the blowers: They had no armor at all to speak of.

As he judged its forward speed the lead craft opened fire. Its turret weapon was a twenty-millimeter Gatling gun. It made a noise like the *wow* of a disc jockey cueing a record magnified a million times.

A section of the swamp just disintegrated. A whirlwind of high explosives stripped away a hundred square meters of vegetation in the blink of an eye. By ill luck the first burst had found the hiding place of part of Sloan's team. Sam saw a man crouching in knee-deep water suddenly come apart like a glass jar dropped on a brick floor, shattered by the impact. The terrible force of the weapon picked up an airboat and flipped it and the occupant backwards, both being shredded by the bullet storm into splintered planks and flaming fuel and streamers of bloody flesh.

Sam's stomach turned inside out. He heard his own airboat pilot throwing up over the side of *'Tit Pichou*, the *Li'l Wildcat*. The Gatling's power strained the hinges of his imagination.

There was going to be no problem getting the rest of his group to fall back; the difficulty was going to be to get them to stop running short of Kansas City. The Gatling uttered its dragon belch again, and he heard a wild shriek, quickly eradicated. His own weapon hung slack in his grip; he brought it up again and fired before his forebrain could come to grips with the possible consequences of making a monster like that mad at him.

The grenade smacked just below the windscreen into the cabin. A lance of vaporized copper impaled the pilot, and the blast must have stunned or injured the gunner, because the multiple barrels, spinning so fast they were a blur, swung off to point to nowhere in particular. Sloan threw himself into the airboat, and his pilot, still retching, peeled it away.

As they roared away a pattern of shells raised a curtain of dirty water off to their right. Some of the Effsee battalion's attached artillery had obviously survived the debacle in Terrebonne Bay.

"Billy—"

"They waited a little too late," his leader's voice came instantly back. "Let's hope that sets a pattern."

• • •

A pattern of sorts had been set. A relief flotilla of airboats, led by young Ron Bouchoux, eager to atone for what he still saw as his own cowardice, swooped to support Sloan's shattered team. Jenny Robidoux flared an Armbrust from *Chouette* and scored a direct hit on the hovercraft Sloan had damaged, which had been quickly brought back under control. All that twenty-millimeter laid on to feed its hungry Gatling made a hell of a fireworks display. That column stopped, just as another one, spearheaded by three more of the shark-mouthed hovercraft, came up on the left flank to take over from the one McKay's team had hit so hard.

McKay had refused to allow the little redhead to be his driver, insisting in his male-chauvinist way that that would be too dangerous for her. So on her own initiative she had attached herself to Ron's tiny squadron, in that way pulling the most hazardous duty of all.

Ron's boat *Maringouin* earned its name as the gray day wore on and Tom Rogers sent them darting from place to place, now to fire a barrage of rockets at the flank of an Effsee advance, there to pick up a handful of frightened rifleman who'd been spotted and fired up by a platoon of Effsees, evacuate them heartbeats ahead of the enemy's called artillery fire.

By noon rain had started to fall sporadically. Lofty columns of black smoke marked the pyres of half a dozen of the Effsees' few precious hovercraft. But at least a score of airboats had been lost, and nobody knew how many of the militia from the bayous.

Despite the casualties, the Acadians and their allies hung grimly in there. Rogers had predicted it; for all their fearsome firepower, the hovercraft were big and vulnerable targets, and the AT rockets produced immediately visible effects when they scored hits. The bayou folk could *see* themselves hurting their enemies, and hurting them badly.

And maybe not as badly as it looked. The real Effsee strength lay in what was still the better part of a battalion of first-rate troops. Their casualties had been light. The Guardians' tactics were geared toward taking out the hovercraft; the antitank rockets, powerful as they were, were virtually useless against personnel, and for civilians armed with nothing heavier than bolt-rifles and a few M-16s, the infantry were actually harder to hurt than the blowers.

The Effsees were getting smarter. It hadn't taken Colonel Correy long to figure out that leading with the hovercraft wasn't working. Now the infantry was out front, riding boats when they could, but just plain wading through the marsh when the boats came under fire. The big blowers hung back, covering the infantry with their rapid-firing guns, blasting pockets of resistance literally out of existence, filling the role that the tube artillery, resting on landfill trucked down from Cocodrie, was simply too slow to accomplish. It was a lethal combination, and the militia's morale was clearly beginning to fray.

Crouched down behind a shock of wire grass, McKay watched three men and a woman flushed from a dense patch of reeds like a covey of quail by one of the Gatlings. None of them made a half dozen steps before being busted like water-balloons full of blood.

"Tom," he said over the communicator, "it's time for Phase II."

"Roger, Billy. Are you still going in?"

"Affirmative."

He could almost taste Rogers's disapproval. But Billy McKay hadn't been made leader of the Guardians in order to be safe from taking risks.

Also, he was eager to start *really* kicking ass.

"Mongol Team Alpha, form up," Rogers's voice ordered over the radio. "Mongol Team Beta, get ready."

McKay sloshed back to where the Falcon kid was waiting, gave him the thumbs-up. The kid grinned. McKay knew he was aching for a chance to show off his prowess as an airboat jockey.

McKay just hoped he'd survive the demonstration.

CHAPTER
SIXTEEN ─────────────

Sam Sloan sat in the squared-off prow of *'Tit Pichou* with his rifle between his knees. To left and right of him stretched a phalanx of a dozen airboats and perhaps twenty conventional powerboats of various sizes. Engines murmured dangerously; the air was charged with ozone crackle that seemed to have nothing to do with the oncoming storm. *Then why do I feel like a sacrificial lamb?* Sloan thought.

Maybe because that was the role this battle line was intended to play—hopefully with negative emphasis on the "sacrificial" part.

"Get ready," Rogers's voice said in his ear. Feeling a little silly, but feeling it was necessary to make some kind of gesture, Sam held his right hand straight up in the air.

"Move out."

Sam whipped his arm down, and the line lunged ahead

like thoroughbreds breaking from the gate.

The action had not surprisingly bogged down along another fairly broad stretch of short grass and open water, tough for either side to cross in the face of heavy fire. Sloan could practically feel the stunned amazement of the Effsees huddled behind their clumps of grass when the whole line broke into the open, screaming like Comanches with their engines full out.

Sloan popped off a frag grenade, broke open the action of the M-203 and crammed in another without waiting to see where the first one landed. This wasn't firing for effect; this was what Billy McKay called busting caps. Some bold souls in the line had volunteered though they were only armed with shotguns, which had about as much chance of doing damage at this range as spitwads. But they did just fine in the sound-and-fury department.

The Effsees did not spend a long time in the shocked and stunned state. Sam Sloan saw muzzle flashes crackle along their own line like heat lightning. Fortunately, in the modern era, marksmanship had been deemphasized, so that the FSE return volley, which looked withering, didn't accomplish a whole hell of a lot. Then the support weapons kicked in—little M-249 Minimi light machine guns spitting like angry kittens, a few full-throated M-60s, the *pop-pop* forty-millimeter grenade launchers. And then here came the main event, the automatic direct-fire guns mounted on the half-dozen hovercraft backing up the rifle line. Sloan's 203 sounded mighty feeble against the howl of incoming fire, but his boat was already breaking to starboard, keeling well over on a brow of greasy water, his driver looking relieved at being able to run from that hell storm without showing cowardice.

And in spite of the plan that had been drummed into everybody's skull, in spite of the constant repetition that the whole *idea* of this exercise was to run away, in spite of the fear of death which was man's oldest and most valuable friend, there were still some who just couldn't bear to show the white feather. The boat next to Sloan's to portside cruised right on ahead, the three occupants blazing merrily away until one of the hovercraft found the range with a Gatling. The effect was like a load of double-ought buck hitting a quail. Sam flinched away from the spray of parts, told himself the idiotic sacrifice would nonetheless foster just the impression they were trying to create, told himself that the warm stuff spattering against his cheek and neck was just another gust of rain. . . .

The militia line was in full retreat. Here and there boats bobbed with their keels turned toward the low-hanging sky, or smoldered in fragments. Survivors of shattered boats ran splashing for the haven of the reeds, while others stood and fired bravely back until they were blown to pieces. In a matter of seconds the attack, which had started with such panache less than a minute before, had simply vanished, blasted back into the tall grass by the Effsee firepower.

"What's happening, Sam?" Rogers asked. "Is it working?" That was the damned thing about Tom Rogers; nobody could possibly fake that total detached calm.

Sam was in the process of earning every penny of his Guardians pay—which was a year in arrears, anyway—all over again. Though the long grass hid them from sight of the enemy, it did not do a lot to slow down the high-explosive twenty-millimeter rounds still reaching out to touch someone from the hovercraft turrets. Instead of fleeing inland far and fast like sensible beings—the way everyone else got to—Sam and pilot Jerry Mattingly were booming along perpendicular to the axis of the fight, headed for the left flank. They had to see what effect their performance had had on the enemy.

Sam reckoned later that what saved them was that old after-the-Holocaust standard, short supplies. The two FSE ships were big enough to carry an awful lot of bullets of various sizes. But your modern battles gobbled ammo like a bulemic pigging out on chocolate-covered cherries. Getting more ammunition from an FSE with troubles of its own was a chancy proposition at best. And once they ran dry, those fearful Gatlings were good for nothing but six-barreled planters.

So almost the instant the attackers faded from view the Effsee commander started screaming at his gunners to cease fire. Otherwise they would certainly have gone ahead and mowed a couple of hectares of coastal marsh to a crewcut in the interests of truth, justice, and Chairman Maximov's way of life. The upshot was that Sloan's boat made it on past the end of the militia line, curved back toward the enemy, and Sam's exhilarated surprise at being alive turned to leaden disappointment.

"They're sitting tight. They're not chasing us. The stupid bastards. What the hell is wrong with them?" In his frustration he was practically shrieking. If the enemy didn't take the bait, then it was all for nothing: lives thrown needlessly away, the last chance to do serious harm to the Effsees vanished, the battle cast like cement in a toe-to-toe slugout that their ragtag army couldn't possibly win. . . .

And then, from off to the southwest, he heard the mosquito whine of a single airboat engine.

"Sarge, c'mon!" Winfield shouted through the gap in his teeth. "We got 'em on the run. Let's go!"

Hunkered down with his M-16 behind a few strands of tall grass, Sergeant Gates frowned at the soldier. "Let's hold off awhile. I got a bad feeling about this."

He had a bad feeling about everything, at this point. He was not a man who enjoyed spending an early-autumn day squatting with his ass in lukewarm soup. Having risen to the exalted rank of sergeant, he had long since learned that the Army didn't much care what he might or might not enjoy. He had also acquired some very well-developed instincts.

Everybody else was whooping and hollering and carrying on. "Look at them coonasses run!" somebody yelled, as the attackers of a moment before went scrambling into the reeds like so many frightened muskrats. The deafening thunder of the blowers' guns was already dying away. Gates could feel his men fidgeting like skittish horses. "Wait for it," he growled.

Then from their left appeared a single airboat, racing bow-high right between the lines at full throttle. A tiny figure in its stern held the tiller with one hand and blasted away with an M-16 on full auto with the other.

It whined halfway down the line before anybody could respond. Then it seemed the entire battalion was cutting loose on the brave, lonely boat, with rifles, grenade launchers, Gatling guns, pistols, thrown rocks, everything. Only Gates, it seemed, held his fire.

For a moment it seemed that the boat would make it anyway. Then it seemed to trip, suddenly went cartwheeling end over end, throwing its pilot far ahead of itself in a spinning sprawl of limbs. Gates caught a glimpse of copper-colored hair, and then the figure splashed into the weeds.

In failure the daring gesture became ludicrous, abruptly bringing home the pathetic nature of the enemy they faced. What was the enemy, after all, but a bunch of half-literate swampers who'd been marrying their own first cousins since shortly after the Battle of the Plains of Abraham? Howling like wolves, the whole FSE line swept forward, some piling into boats, others just taking off on foot through the swamp, lusting to be in at the kill.

Sergeant Gates bellowed at his men, trying to hold them

back from the general rush to hot pursuit. It didn't work. Men who over a year and more had learned the value of listening to the sergeant forgot to listen to him now in the moment's hot rush.

"Didn't anybody see that was a woman?" he asked nobody in particular.

"Shit, Sergeant," said Private Luttrell, "what the hell kind of men are they, they got to send out women to do their fighting for them?"

Then he was bounding off, splashing to join the rest. Gates bared his teeth. *I got better control of my men than this.* But the madness had affected the whole line; no way to hang back now. Feeling grim premonition, he trudged forward.

As the FSE troops swept forward, cheering at the top of their lungs, Mongol Team Beta swung into action.

Out of sight beyond the tall grass twenty airboats drove at full throttle around the right flank of the charging mob of Effsees. These were the men—and a few women—personally picked by Rogers, with the help of Black Jacques, as the finest shots and the steadiest hands. With them went almost all the remaining antitank rockets.

McKay rode the lead craft, one hand holding his lightweight M-60, the other white-knuckle locked on the gunwale. He'd never ridden one of these things going balls-to-the-wall before. It was quite an experience. The only thing he could think of to compare it to would be trying to ride a jet-powered sled down a washboard road. Each and every jar threatened to spring his kidneys loose, and a constant spray of water flew up in his face.

It was just the sort of thing Casey would love, and Casey did, to judge from the ear-splitting rebel yells McKay could hear from several boats back even above the manic shriek of the engines—thoughtfully, Casey had cut his communicator before venting his exuberance. They were going to be lucky if Casey didn't insist on keeping one of the frigging things, and carrying it around strapped to the top of Mobile One like a surfboard.

It was asking a lot of the Falcon boy, having him trailblaze the whole operation. He came through like a champion. The boat swerved sickeningly around another bend in the channel following and then abruptly swerved again to avoid running into a launch loaded with Effsee troops, putting forward to reinforce the battleline.

Unflinching, Falcon drove on. McKay twisted, trying to brace himself with his legs, raked the launch with a single ripping burst as the airboat flashed alongside. He saw faces, mouths open in *O*'s of astonishment beneath helmets; saw bodies tumbling across one another as people tried to get out of the way of his bullets; saw blood. Then the airboat was past, roaring down another channel that led to starboard, behind the half-dozen hovercraft supporting the Effsee advance. From behind he heard the popping of more shots as the rest of the column screamed by the unfortunate boat.

Suddenly the grass was growing shorter, unfolding the whole scene before McKay's eyes. The big blowers were horrifyingly close, the backs of a couple of hundred men visible beyond them as the enemy soldiers rushed forward in pursuit of the fleeing Mongol Team Alpha. Chalk up another one to Tom Rogers; he'd borrowed this little scheme from the Golden Horde, and it had worked out just as slick as could be.

At this range the pounding of McKay's M-60 had overridden the sound of the boats and the hovercraft's own gigantic fans. The second in line, showing quicker reflexes than the others, was turning in a swirl of mud and water to bring its front turret to bear on this unexpected attack from the rear. The Gatling screamed like a banshee. Glancing over his shoulder past the cage that enclosed *Minou Noir*'s fan he saw three airboats and their occupants vanish in a storm of explosions.

He chopped his arm down violently. At the prearranged signal, Achille toed-in toward the Effsees, bringing the craft broadside, letting the mud-heavy water brake them to a stop. McKay pitched the sandbag that his boat carried onto the weeds growing from some mud that humped up a couple of centimeters above the surface. He jumped after it, leaving his chopper for the moment in favor of the fat fiberglass tube of an Armbrust. Agile as waterbugs, other airboats scooted by him to take up positions farther on.

The Gatling howled again. McKay was too busy preparing his weapon to see if any more airboats were hit. He hoped to hell Casey had made it. But the kid was on his own, just like the rest of them. He rested the launcher on his shoulder and fired.

It was a clean shot. It hit the hovercraft amidships and set it on fire. McKay dropped the spent launcher, grabbed his machine gun, threw down the bipod and then went face first in the muck, propping the weapon on the sandbag. As more rockets streaked toward the blowers, he began cranking laddered bursts into the charging Effsees from behind.

Out in the open men began to fall. Others of Mongol Team Beta were spilling out of their airboats, firing up the Effsees, touching off their big AT rockets. Men died, hovercraft exploded. Grimly, McKay hosed the distant soldiers with the powerful machine gun.

It was a tiny attack, totally insignificant—except for one thing. Nothing freaks the squaddies out quicker or more completely than being hit with a sudden savage attack from the rear. The disproportionate effect of the last-ditch volley of AT rockets at barely a hundred meters' range pumped the impression that the Effsees were caught in the kill zone; three of the hovercraft were burning like torches or blowing up, the rest milling in confusion.

The Effsees packed it in. The victorious headlong advance of the FSE troopers changed with heart-attack suddenness into rout as their morale dissolved.

"Casey . . . Black Jack?" To his relief both acknowledged. "We got them on the run—let's get out of here!"

He came up to his knees, waving his arms and roaring, "Move! Everybody, get gone!" at the top of his lungs.

An airboat skidded flamboyantly up like a skier banking to a halt in snow fifteen meters from McKay. It was *Maringouin*. Ron Bouchoux sat at the tiller, alone and triumphant. He gave McKay a thumbs-up, his teeth very white beneath his mustache.

A twenty mike-mike shell blew apart *Maringouin*'s feathered prop and its cage. A second exploded Ron's rib cage. The burst walked on past McKay and Achille, raising five-meter geysers of muddy water just behind *Black Cat*.

McKay threw himself into the boat and they got the hell out of there with McKay scattering shots at the frantic Effsee troops streaming back for the beachhead. This battle was won.

Unfortunately, one battle wasn't the whole campaign. The Effsees had taken heavy casualties, but not enough to stop them, not with Colonel Correy's iron determination to drive them onward to Wolf Bayou.

Overnight the militia withdrew into the cypress swamps, taking their own wounded with them. These included Jenny Robidoux, who miraculously had suffered no harm worse than a broken leg from having her boat shot from beneath her and being catapulted through the air at thirty miles an hour at the end of her little joyride.

"I told you to keep the fuck out of trouble!" McKay

bellowed at her, when he came up to the impromptu aid station underneath the willow where Tom was just finishing setting her leg. She merely grinned and gave him the finger.

It wasn't as if the defenders expected the Effsees to give up, not most of them, anyway. The militia partied hearty that night, and some of the younger or more impression-able thought the fight had settled things for good and all. But the older hands knew better.

Next morning the Effsees advanced again, far more dis-persed than previously, hungering for a rematch. The first hovercraft to poke its blunt snout up a bayou was levitated five meters into the air and tossed into a stand of cypress by a humongous charge of dynamite laid and command-detonated by Tom Rogers himself. Another love tap from the defenders, good for another wrecked blower, another handful of casualties, another delay.

Inexorably, the FSE battalion pushed on. The Cajuns made the advance hell. The narrow bayous with their banks overgrown with vegetation made ideal ambush country. The militia could blaze suddenly away from point-blank range, and fade away before any of the survivors could shoot back—or just pick off the invaders one at a time, using the low-velocity and thoroughly illegal rifles with homemade silencers some of the more accomplished bayou poachers favored. The Effsees fought for every centimeter they gained.

But they gained. Rogers and McKay, with Weygand and a few others, had understood that the first day's battle would be the last pitched fight. The militia would mount no more all-out attacks; their victory had cost them dearly, in lives, in boats, in bullets. All they could do was harry the invaders in hopes of convincing them theirs was a hopeless task.

• • •

Three days after the fight in the marsh, the sky turned a peculiar shade of yellow and the rain began to fall. The word crackled up the bayous like electric current: *hurricane coming*.

The militia came apart at the seams as the bayou folk sought what shelter they could find against the approaching storm. They suggested the Guardians do likewise.

"What's the big deal?" McKay scoffed. "Shit, we're forty klicks inland."

"Billy," the other three Guardians said at once. They were in what had been a camp of about thirty people, in a fairly solid clearing among a stand of tupelo gum and hackberry trees. The locals were vanishing quicker than teens in a slasher flick.

June-Marie got the floor. "The plague killed the most people, but what do you think scoured away so many signs that the people had been here at all? The developers were in the bayou country long before the war. Much of it was still wild—now almost all of it is again. Thank the hurricanes."

"Well, I—" McKay stammered, for once at a loss for words.

"The hurricanes after the war wiped everything out. If you haven't lived through one"—she shook her head—"then you don't really know what hell is."

They got an invitation to hole up at the home of Black Jacques Weygand himself, up on the fringe of the Atchafalaya Swamp proper. They made the run in a pair of boats piloted by Jenny, her leg in a cast, and Casey Wilson, who was so excited about finally being able to drive one of the damned things that he all but forgot about the way the sky kept getting yellower and yellower and was beginning to churn like something from a Steven Spielberg flick.

The Weygand house was two stories tall, larger and better kept up than the Falcon house, set on a fairly substantial rise of ground. As they trudged up from the landing, McKay helping to support the diminutive Jenny, a sound broke from the woods that glistened darkly on all sides of them.

They stood frozen in place. It was a strange sound, a terrible sound, a rising-falling wail with the urgency of an air-raid siren but without its regularity. A million voices raised in a weird beating-heart harmony. It rose up as if from the moist earth around them and seemed to vibrate in their bones.

"Jesus Christ," McKay said, "what's *that?*"

"It's the birds," June-Marie said. "All the birds in the whole swamp country, crying out at once."

McKay felt ice water down the back of his neck, even though the rain was warm as blood.

"It's just what Whitey told us," marveled Sam Sloan. A fresh onslaught of rain sent them scurrying for the house.

And then the storm burst upon the swampland like a hydrogen bomb.

CHAPTER
SEVENTEEN ——————————

Sergeant Gates was trapped in a nightmare. He was wet right through, his helmet gone. The sky was brown and black, the rain slashed in parallel to water which had risen within moments to their waists, and the noise sounded as if he were lying on his belly on a railroad track while a freight train rushed on and on overhead. The wind was so ferocious he could not stand upright against it. He clung to a cypress tree shaking his head as though he'd been beaten.

"Sergeant." Though Hawthorn had his mouth next to Gates's ear he was barely audible above the hurricane's rage. "We got to do something! We'll drown!" A flash of lightning silvered the ashen fear of his complexion.

Gates caught his own panic and strangled it. The squad was facing an enemy like none it had ever known. An enemy no courage or cunning would defeat. That meant fear was a luxury he couldn't afford.

"The trees," he screamed back. "Belt yourselves to the trees. Shinny up while the water rises—try to keep above it—"

Holding his helmet on top of his white-blond hair Luttrell tried to run between trees to where Gates clung. A wall of wind caught him up and flung him through the air like a discarded milk carton. He hit across the bole of a cypress with a crack audible above the hideous roar, splashed into the churned water, and never came up.

With numb fingers Gates unfastened his belt, resecured it around the base of his own tree like a lineman's belt, began to shinny up. The squad would have to just follow his example; you couldn't pass orders in *this*. As he did so the roots of a live oak not fifteen meters from him gave way and the tree came smashing down right on top of little round Sanchez and the commo pack.

We're in your hands, Lord, he thought, and climbed like hell.

With a mixture of awe and horror Captain Mancuso watched a wave pick up a hovercraft and throw it in among the trees as if it were a scale model by Revell. A wave howled over the gunwales of his own small vessel, almost tore him loose.

Ahead of him LST 1179 bobbed madly on a sea gone berserk. The fury of the hurricane was greater than he had imagined, greater than anything he could have imagined. *If the anchor chains part we're done for,* he thought.

Behind him Colonel Enos Correy himself manned the tiller of the launch, jaw set, bareheaded in the storm. The boat was laden well past what was safe on the calmest day with wounded men from the infirmary in Cocodrie. But there was no choice. Each storm since the One-Day War had torn away more of the little town, and this one seemed determined to finish it off for good and all. Whipped by the awful winds the waters of the bay surged through the town, literally scouring buildings from their moorings.

There were civilians huddled among the moaning injured men. Correy had ordered as many of them evacuated as the little flotilla of launches and lifeboats would permit. The journey past the *Marshall*'s grave to the storm-tossed LST was insanely dangerous—even as he swiped what seemed like gallons of seawater from his eyes Mancuso saw a gigantic wave break over a boat forty meters to port and completely swamp it—but even horrific risk was better than the certain death on the shore that was being devoured by the sea.

The battalion was dying. Though their progress toward the Atchafalaya had been steady since the first day's fiasco, Correy had been subdued the last few days. "We're stalemated," he said. "And in this country, at this time of year, stalemate favors the defenders." He wouldn't amplify, and his complexion was so gray, the flesh on his face beginning to sag from its former granite firmness, that Mancuso had been afraid to press. But now he knew what the colonel meant: this was hurricane country and hurricane season. If the swampers delayed them long enough, a storm could come and win their battle for them.

It had and it was. The launch came over the top of a wave and slammed headlong into the *Newport*'s steel-gray flank. For one adrenal moment Mancuso feared the bow was stove in, that they would go to the bottom within fingertip reach of safety, but then they were riding alongside the ship, while lines and ladders dropped among them, and Royal Navy bluejackets in lifevests came swarming down.

Even in the lee of the bigger ship Mancuso couldn't

stand upright. He held on as best he could while he helped the sailors dog lines around wounded men. If they were too badly hurt to battle up the ladders unassisted they were hauled bodily up, bumping along the hull, and if they didn't survive that treatment they were no deader than they would have been left behind. For a young officer from headquarters staff, who'd never experienced a real battle, it was a soul-searing experience.

With a thin cry a scrawny woman in a sodden pink nightgown vanished overboard. The baby she had cradled in her arms bobbed briefly on the surface just aft of the stern. Correy threw himself into the water, clawing for the child. Mancuso hurled himself after him, grabbed him by the leg of his trousers as the baby vanished in a roil of water. Correy was weeping openly as sailors dragged them both back into the boat.

"Everyone's aboard, Colonel," an ensign shouted. "Come along quickly now, if you please."

Correy shook him off. "Still people ashore. I'm going back."

"Colonel, no!" Mancuso yelled.

"Take him aboard."

"No—I'm coming with you—"

The colonel drove a punch against the point of Mancuso's blue-tinged jaw. White lights went off in his brain, and he sagged into the waiting arms of the bluejackets. They bustled him to a rope ladder as Correy settled himself down at the tiller again. His limbs would not respond. He was pulled up by unseen hands above.

The launch growled away from the big ship. Mancuso pulled loose from the seamen crowding around. The landing ship lurched crazily beneath his feet. "Come away, sir, you'll go over the railing," someone cried.

A monster wave caught up Correy's launch, flung it into

the air. For an instant Mancuso watched it cartwheel end-for-end, the tiny figure of a man spinning beside it. Then both splashed down to be driven deep by another wall of water.

They had to drag Mancuso below and lash him in a bunk.

It was over. And not just the storm. In the parlor of the Falcon house, its floor still awash with mud—but a damned sight drier than anything south of it—Billy McKay accepted the surrender of the remnant of the Effsee forces from a young captain named Mancuso, who would have been offensively handsome if he hadn't looked as if he had just been let out of hell on a day pass.

Colonel Enos Correy was dead, along with half his command; McKay learned he had drowned while trying to get the wounded off the rapidly flooding beachhead to the comparative safety of LST 1179.

The bayous had suffered too. Men who had distinguished themselves by their bravery not days before drowned like rats in the storm. But the bayou people knew how to endure, how to bend with the hurricane's force. Though Billy McKay personally still felt as if he'd been tied by the feet and used as the clapper of a bell as he signed the document scrawled on the back of an old manila envelope. When the water started lapping at the second floor landing of the Weygand house, he had been sure that This Was It.

The surrender signed, the Guardians left the bayou folk and former enemies to sort things out as best they could while the flood waters slowly receded. They themselves had business northwest—on Wolf Bayou.

Kettle Belly Calhoun came to meet them as they walked up from the cement pier: the Guardians, June-Marie, and

Jenny Robidoux, who with Casey Wilson had piloted their two power boats. The Project Starshine leader's well-weathered face was grim.

"So you won."

McKay stopped, faced him, took his cigar out of his face. "Yeah."

Calhoun shook his head. "Perhaps it would have been better if you hadn't. Come on, let's go inside." He turned and walked back toward the block house that concealed the entrance to the underground facility.

Burning scarlet flush began to creep up the back of McKay's neck, overtaking his ears and flooding into his face. The muscles of neck and jaw bunched. June-Marie laid a hand on his arm. "Take it easy, Lieutenant McKay. He is a difficult man. He always tries to do absolutely what he considers right; that's why he's so difficult."

McKay produced an inarticulate rumble deep in his throat. Then he led the way after Calhoun.

"Mr. President," Calhoun said in his gravel voice, "I have to tell you in all honesty that I have grave misgivings over your fitness as a steward for the power which Project Starshine represents."

McKay was turning red again. Rogers and Sloan sat on either side of him, ready to intercept him if his temper got the better of him and he made a move for the grizzled scientist.

The secret of Starshine was right in the palms of their hands; even if the facility's personnel managed to destroy the records—as a worst-case scenario—Blueprint experts under the aegis of Lee Warwick would be able to piece out the workings of the fusion reactor, deduce the theoretical breakthroughs and technological innovations that made it work. But that would add months, possibly years of delay in bringing Starshine's benefits to war-ravaged America.

America needed Starshine now, and could only have it with the assistance of the people who had brought it into existence. And it was hardly the kind of assistance that could be gained from people by sticking guns against their heads. Like so many of the people involved with Blueprint projects whom the Guardians had encountered, the personnel of Wolf Bayou were fanatically devoted to their charismatic if curmudgeonly leader. The Guardians still had to tread warily here.

They were sitting in an up-to-the-minute communications center, which, unlike Calhoun's cramped office, did not date from the place's days as an ammunition dump. It was spacious and carpeted, equipped with banks of consoles and equipment only slightly less awe-inspiring than that in the actual command center, which looked for all the world like the bridge of TV's Starship *Enterprise*.

"That needle-nosed son of a bitch," McKay said, his *voice* not all that *sotto*. "He had all this fancy-assed gear and scrambler equipment. He could have fucking *called* us in Heartland. We coulda had all this"—he swept his big scarred hand around in a gesture that encompassed the entire facility beyond the soundproofed walls of the room—"the minute the all-clear sounded."

"The Blueprint people were told, like, to lay low until we came for them," pointed out Casey Wilson, sprawled on a chair to one side.

"Maybe just as well he kept his peace," added Rogers. "Otherwise, the Effsees would have Apollo now."

"—nothing against you personally, sir; I intend no disrespect. I'm sure you are a fine man. But I must question whether you possess the firmness of character, the wisdom necessary to best apply our discovery to the benefit of our nation and mankind—"

It was getting too much for McKay in here. He lunged

up out of his chair. Rogers and Sloan popped up as if they were all marionettes attached to the same set of strings, but instead of going for Calhoun he went for the door. Outside on the bare cement landing he stood panting as if he'd run ten miles. He wanted to puke.

"We've won, McKay," said Sloan, coming out behind him. "We may not like Dr. Calhoun—but then again, we don't have to. You're the one who's always telling us the mission is everything. Well—mission accomplished. One way or another."

McKay nodded convulsively. "Yeah. You're right, Navy boy. Much as it gripes my ass to admit it."

Sloan looked thoughtfully at the closed door to the comm center. "I have to admit our esteemed Dr. Calhoun seems to be displaying megalomaniacal tendencies."

"Shit. The thought of him talking to President Jeff like that—" McKay forced himself to stop before he got a full head of steam.

"Just wait until Angie's mom gets on the line, man," Casey said with a grin. "*She'll* tell him a few things."

McKay smiled. "I never thought it was possible," he said. "We've found somebody who actually *deserves* Maggie Connoly."

Calhoun's little speech delivered, arrangements were begun for Blueprint scientists to come down and begin working on the practical problems of getting Starshine's power output online. The Tide Campers were sent off to see if they could round up a salvageable plane to bring them down in. Meanwhile the Guardians had lots of nothing to do but loaf around the quarters Calhoun had grudgingly given them and bitch about the state of the world.

Sam was outraged that Calhoun had not found some way to use the facility to benefit at least the people of the swamp and bayou country during the terrible hardships that had followed the war. To his dismay, McKay found himself defending the doctor; the secret of Starshine was simply too vital to take the least chance word of it might leak out to the wrong parties. Even the harshness of the methods Calhoun had used to maintain absolute secrecy—making the name of Wolf Bayou synonymous with terror and mysterious death—McKay could see the point behind.

On the other hand, he didn't have much of an answer for Sloan's and Casey's contentions that Calhoun and the sizable Starshine staff could have found some way to help their neighbors without compromising security.

It had been pretty much that issue that caused laser technician June-Marie Landry to walk away from Project Starshine during the worst of the plagues that followed the One-Day War. As a brilliant martinet of a boss, she had found him a tolerable, even in a perverse way inspirational, man to work for. As absolute ruler of the destinies of the facility personnel during the nightmare days after the war —and would-be arbiter of the destiny of all mankind—she found him much harder to take.

She had believed then, and insisted now to Sloan, that Calhoun's isolating Wolf Bayou behind a curtain of fear and mystery had little to do with security. "He loves living here in his godlike isolation, biding his time. Before I left he used to say that Starshine was a lever big enough to move the world; all he needed was a fulcrum. Watch out for him, Sam. I think this Chairman Maximov might look like a far bigger fulcrum than your President MacGregor."

Two days later McKay and Sloan were getting an extended version of the quick tour they'd had on their first visit. McKay was already getting restless and bored, and the air of scarcely repressed hostility toward the Guardians was thick enough to cut with a knife. However, the egotism of an inventor had overcome Calhoun's reservations about the winners of the Starshine sweepstakes. He was explaining the details of his creation with not-unjustified pride. It was a measure of McKay's boredom that he was listening.

"—problem in finding a substance to use in suspending the lithium deuteride pellet in the focus of the laser beams. All the metals we tried were too dense, had too much mass when the filaments we used were thick enough to have sufficient tensile strength to hold the pellets as the reaction began. The filaments would begin to be vaporized by the beams and interfere with the reaction. Do you know what we eventually wound up using?"

Sloan shook his head. "Bubblegum?" McKay grunted.

"Spider silk. Its tensile strength is enormous."

Sloan shook his head. "Amazing. What you've accomplished here is truly a magnificent achievement, Doctor."

Calhoun nodded heavily. "I cannot overestimate the importance that this breakthrough be utilized in the most efficient way for humanity." He sat in a swivel-mounted pedestal chair, turned it to face them. "Gentlemen, let me ask you one question: Do you really, in your hearts, feel that your President MacGregor commands the ability and the resources to make the maximal use of Starshine?"

Sloan's eyes narrowed. "You wouldn't be suggesting we turn our coats, now, would you, Doctor?"

"I'm asking you to consider whether your loyalty doesn't belong first to all mankind."

"Our first loyalty belongs to *America*, Doctor," Sam said pointedly. "Have you forgotten that this entire project was made possible by the Blueprint for Renewal, explicitly for the purpose of rebuilding our country?"

Calhoun gestured through the observation window at the squat, glistening metal doughnut of the generator reactor.

"Commander Sloan, such power transcends—"

It was too much for Billy McKay. "Power!" he exploded. "That's fuckin' what it's all about, ain't it, Doctor? And I don't mean the kind of power that goes into light bulbs and electric toothbrushes. I mean the other kind of power, like an emperor has.

"That's what this goddamn Project Starshine means to you. You see it as some kind of—some kind of wild card, and all you're waiting for is to be dealt the right hand for you to rake in all the chips."

Calhoun's lips were a bloodless line. "My interest is the interest of all mankind."

McKay smirked. "Yeah. Keep sayin' that, Doc. You might even make yourself believe it someday."

The intercom buzzed for attention. Calhoun shook himself, reached over to stab a button with a liver-spotted finger. "What is it?"

"Doctor," stammered the voice of one of Calhoun's eager young aides—acolytes, June-Marie called them. "We're receiving a transmission from a man who claims to be the captain of a warship in Atchafalaya Bay."

"Yes? Well, woman, what does he say?"

"He says that if you do not surrender Project Starshine to him immediately, he'll destroy the facility with missiles!"

CHAPTER
EIGHTEEN ─────────────

"I shall repeat what I told your communications officer, Dr. Calhoun," the voice said from the radio when Kettle Belly had identified himself. It was a beautifully modulated baritone voice, which spoke precise if heavily accented English. "I am Commander Rafael Asusta, captain of the People's Revolutionary frigate, *Cienfuegos*. I am giving you precisely twenty-four hours from this moment—eleven hundred thirteen hours your time, by my chronometer, Doctor—to surrender your facility to me in the name of the Revolution. Otherwise, I shall be forced to destroy it in order to deny it to the forces of global imperialism."

Sloan pushed forward, mimed at the mike. Calhoun surrendered it. "This is Commander Sam Sloan, formerly of the United States Navy. I've seen your ship. Your SS-N-23s are antishipping missiles. How do you propose to use them against a land target?"

"Well informed as you are, Commander, you naturally know that the missiles have a fifty-kilometer range, which a glance at a map will convince you is ample. They are surface-to-surface missiles; there is no magical reason they won't work over land. We will simply program them with the proper range and bearing, and launch them, trusting that their nose radars will pick up a suitably prominent target to fix on for terminal guidance. Such as that very squat silo of yours."

The voice chuckled. Asusta was clearly imagining the dumbstruck silence his bombshell had brought to the communications center. "You see, Commander Sloan, you're not the only one to conduct on-the-spot surveillance. The disruption caused by the flooding provided an excellent opportunity for Comrade Sergeant Maestre and his Guard Flotilla scouts to penetrate Wolf Bayou and get an excellent look at your facility."

"How the hell did you find out about us?" Calhoun demanded, roughly seizing the mike.

"Well, Commander Sloan," an all-too-familiar voice said, "I guess you might just say we meet again. For your benefit, Dr. Calhoun, I'm John Myers, formerly of the Central Intelligence Agency and until recently a political officer for the Federated States of Europe."

Calhoun's jaw dropped. "You mean you sold out first your own country and then the FSE?" he choked.

"You're a fine one to talk, Doc," mumbled McKay. Calhoun gave him a bleak look.

Myers chuckled. "Well, gosh, I guess you might just say I made a realistic accommodation to a change in circumstances."

"It's a crazy scheme," said Luc Landry. "It'll never work."

They were in some sort of briefing hall or conference

room in the bowels of the Starshine facility. McKay looked at Tom Rogers. "Well, you're right," the former Marine said. "It is a crazy idea. But it's the only thing that has a chance of working."

"You are seriously considering trying to sneak aboard this Cuban frigate?" Calhoun demanded incredulously.

"Billy's got experience in that line," Rogers said. "The rest of us—" He shrugged. "We think we can give it a try."

"With what chance of success?" Landry demanded. Tom just smiled.

"There's something I don't understand," Calhoun said, as if the admission hurt him. "Captain Asusta—Commander, whatever—never once referred to himself or his ship as 'Cuban.' Why is that?"

"Yeah, Major Crenna's intelligence indicated our bomber strike destroyed the Cuban navy at anchor," Casey said. "And the stuff we got from—that is, our own intelligence sources monitoring the Cubans never gave a hint they still have anything like this missile frigate."

Sam, who knew a lot of naval history, looked thoughtful. "I think what we've got here is a sort of one-ship revolutionary government-in-exile. It's happened before, back in—May of 1877, I believe. I think that *Cienfuegos* is a ship without a country, and her captain intends to do something about carving one out for her."

"That's weird," McKay said.

"So? What *hasn't* been weird, these last fifteen months?"

"To return to the subject at hand, gentlemen—" Calhoun prodded.

Chewing on her underlip, June-Marie Landry rested the first two fingers of her left hand on the USGS map of Atchafalaya Bay spread out on the table. "Didn't some of the howitzers the FSE had in Terrebonne Bay survive? Perhaps we could move them up under cover and use them.

There's patches of fairly firm land that ought to be within range of the ship."

McKay was frowning, mainly because he still wasn't any too used to allowing women to sit in on councils of war. But June-Marie and Jenny were both on hand, since, among other things, they were bona fide experts on the terrain in question.

"Then she'd just move out of range," Sloan said. "Her missiles would still have plenty of legs to reach Wolf Bayou. Those dinky little 105s wouldn't have enough punch to cripple her before she got away from them."

"I could take *Werewolf*," Landry offered. *Werewolf* was the name of Project Starshine's field-expedient flying saucer; shortage of ego had never been a problem here in Wolf Bayou, it seemed. "I could strafe her with the laser."

"You can carry what? Three shots at a time?" McKay asked.

"Four."

"Great. So you hover in their line of sight and manually switch the system from cartridge to cartridge between shots. I don't care if your little UFO does have low-infrared-signature engines and radar-jamming gear up the wazoo—those Cubans're gonna find a way to put a missile in you. They'll have what you call incentive."

"That laser's death on choppers," Sloan said, "but is it enough to take out a frigate in four shots?"

Landry showed teeth through a mouth turned down at the corners and said nothing.

"Sorry, *Loup-Garou*," Casey said, grinning. "Looks like we handle this one." Inevitably a friendly rivalry had grown up between them, the best fixed-wing and the best rotary-wing pilots in the world.

"Great, we got that settled," McKay said. "Now, Doc, you got a fair amount of dynamite stashed away here, for construction work and keeping Mother Nature at bay?"

Calhoun nodded; of course they did. "Fine. And here's the plan. Tommy'll make up some hefty satchel charges in waterproof cases. We'll pack them suckers aboard—"

"You really intend to go through with it?" Calhoun cut him off incredulously.

"Uh-huh."

"And what chances do you give yourself to succeed?"

A lopsided grin: "Slim and none, Doc. To be wildly optimistic."

Calhoun shut his eyes. "I can see that I have badly misjudged you, Lieutenant McKay. You and your men."

"Fucking-A straight, Doc. Big of you to admit it."

"Well, fuck me to tears," Billy McKay said, peering out through the twilit reeds.

"It shall be done," promised Sam Sloan.

He was right. It looked as if Christmas in Central Park had magically been transported through space and time to right spang in the middle of Atchafalaya Bay. The frigate blazed with lights until she practically resembled *Werewolf* in her flying saucer drag.

Even at several hundred meters' distance, the Guardians could clearly see men moving about her decks. It didn't take binoculars to know they'd be wearing the camouflage of the Guard Flotilla, the Cuban Marines.

"Looks like they're having a party," Casey remarked, "and, we're, like, expected to show."

"Well, fuck Asusta with an ICBM, anyway," McKay said. "He's too smart for his own good."

"Or ours," Casey said.

Sam sighed. "Well, shoot. I was *so* looking forward to crossing PO Myers's path again."

McKay rubbed his jaw. "Well, I guess this blows rowing

out there in pirogues with our faces painted black and knives in our teeth and playing Cockleshell Heroes."

"We could forget about the satchel charges and try to swim out there, see if we could climb up her anchor chain," Rogers mused.

Jeannette Robidoux, sitting in the airboat with her gimpy leg propped up, could hold her tongue no longer. "That's ridiculous! What are your chances of getting away with a stunt like that?"

Rogers shrugged. "Well, I guess Billy called them pretty accurately, back at the bayou."

"This is crazy," June-Marie said from the airboat bobbing next to Jenny's. "Why throw your lives away?"

"Because there's a tiny fraction of a chance we might avoid having to choose between losing Starshine either to the Cubans or their missiles," Sam said softly. "And because we're Guardians."

Tears in her eyes, June-Marie shook her head. She knew better than to try to argue further.

Jeannette was something different. "Now, listen, you great big heroes. Can't you think of doing anything but swimming out there and gnawing on that big iron boat like beavers? *Merde*. If you'd just try thinking with your heads instead of your—"

A green line split the sky.

Sparks coruscated from the base of a mast radar on the forward superstructure. It toppled in slow motion, carrying with it a guyline festooned with lights. Excited yells from the deck carried clearly across the still water of the bay.

June-Marie spun, making the boat rock dangerously. *"Luc!"*

A whispering cruciform shadow hung half a kilometer to their right: *Werewolf*, stripped of her Mylar cloak. The Guardians saw small orange muzzle flashes as the Guard

Flotilla opened up with their AKMs. A bigger flame billowed from the after superstructure as a 12.7-mm began to chug. Barrels spectral-pale in the failing light, the 100-millimeters in their turrets began to traverse landward.

The green brilliance stabbed out again, struck another rain of sparks from the base of the superstructure like flint on steel. The X-turret gun boomed. The shell moaned overhead and exploded somewhere in the swamp behind. A moment later the Y gun fired too.

June-Marie had her eyes squeezed tightly shut, was slowly beating on her bluejeaned thighs with her fists. Casey's fingers were locked on the gunwales, and he swiveled his head back and forth, almost frantically.

"He's crazy, man!" Casey yelled. "He can't do it. He'll never make it!"

A SAM hissed away from its launcher. McKay felt his guts fist into a knot as the missiles streaked straight for the verti. At the last moment it darted upward, engines whining into audibility. The missile flashed harmlessly past beneath.

The laser winked again. The port twelve-barreled anti-submarine launcher flared, then the whole front of the vessel lit up as the little rockets gangfired. The onlookers cheered.

There were at least two of the big 12.7s at work now, hosing streams of green tracers. One of them swept across the *Werewolf*. The pilot reacted too late; the watchers saw several quick firefly flashes of hits on the fuselage and wings.

June-Marie moaned.

The last laser shot hit the humped emplacement housing the lethal SS-N-23 launchers. Sparks sprayed in muted counterpoint to the show put on by the exploding antisubmarine launcher. Sloan grabbed McKay's arm. "Look—

those flames. The solid fuel of one of the missiles has caught!"

"Will she blow, take out the whole rig?"

Sloan's face looked suddenly old in the light of distant fires. "Not if their damage-control parties are on the ball."

McKay took out a cigarette, struck a match and puffed it alight, held it up in salute to the distant aircraft. "Well, buddy, nice try."

As if in reply, the verti's engines sang with full-throttle power.

"How bad is the fire, Comrade Cardenas?" Asusta said. He held Neruda in the crook of his left arm, scratching the fat little dog behind the ears. Neruda wagged his tail appreciatively.

The executive officer, nattily groomed as always, turned away from a speaker. "Bad, but damage control reports they'll have it under control before it endangers the other missiles."

Standing at the captain's side in a bridge lit only by the psychedelic glow of instrument displays, Myers shook his head. "This is ridiculous. What kind of an idiot is that, anyway, pulling a stunt like this?"

Asusta took a cigar from the breast pocket of his uniform tunic. He would not light it in here, out of consideration for the bridge crew, which mostly meant Cardenas. "Actually, I think he is quite brave. On the other hand, I have the feeling he's shot his wad, as I believe you Americans would put it. If he had another shot, he would have fired it by now."

Two streams of green tracers converged on the distant aircraft. "Why doesn't he run?" Cardenas demanded.

"He's moving!" somebody on the bridge yelled.

"There he goes," Myers said smugly.

"But, Comrade Captain—he's headed right for us!"

Asusta raised an eyebrow. He smiled. "Comrade Cardenas, pass the word to abandon ship."

Cardenas looked at him, dumbstruck. "The comrade captain jests!"

Two more SAMS whooshed away. Neither came close. By now the others on the bridge could clearly see the hybrid aircraft coming toward them, gathering speed. "Do it. We don't have the firepower to stop him, this close."

As the speakers blared the warning to abandon ship Myers stared at Asusta in consternation. "What is this, some kind of joke?"

"A joke on us. Cardenas, what are you doing still here?"

The exec jutted his bearded jaw. "I'm staying."

"If you disobey a direct order, I'll shoot you. In the name of the Revolution, and our friendship—*go.*"

His face streaming tears, the lieutenant turned to join the bridge crew stampeding down the ladder to the deck. "Cardenas."

At the hatch the exec turned. Asusta kissed Neruda on the top of his round little head, tossed the dog underhand to Cardenas. The exec barely caught him. The animal struggled, windmilling his stumpy legs, rolling his bug eyes frantically for his master.

"Find him a good home, old friend," Asusta said. Cardenas couldn't speak. He bobbed his head, vanished down the ladder.

Most of the exchange had taken place in Spanish. But Myers was not slow on the uptake. He started to dart for the hatchway too. Asusta's hand fastened on his arm like a steel claw. "Where do you think you're going?"

Wide-eyed, the blond political officer pointed at the aircraft swelling rapidly in the windscreen. "We've got to get out of here!" he screamed, spittle flying from his bloodless lips.

Asusta stuck the cigar in his mouth, lit it. "That's a hero, there. We can't let him show us up, now, can we?"

And he threw back his bearded head, and was laughing a laugh fit for legend when *Werewolf*, loaded with aviation fuel and several hundred kilograms of dynamite from the Starshine stocks, smashed into the bridge at four hundred kilometers an hour.

Even from the shore it was apparent that the Cuban captain had been right to order abandon-ship. The verti's kamikaze attack blasted the entire forward superstructure into blazing, twisted ruin and sent flaming fuel sluicing across the decks like lava.

"She's doomed," Sloan said in a thick voice. "She'll never survive that."

The rumble of the first of what promised to be many secondary explosions rolled across the water, lending emphasis to his words. Sloan unfolded himself from the airboat, swung his legs over the side, splashed to the other. Standing to his waist in the womb-warm water, he put his arms around the sobbing June-Marie.

EPILOGUE ————————————

"I am a pilot without an aircraft," Captain Luc Landry, late of the United States Army, said sourly.

"So we'll get you a new one somewhere," McKay said. He gestured at the squad of men drawn up beside the blockhouse in the hot morning sunshine. "Until then, you can have fun bossing around Project Starshine's new security team."

Sergeant Horatio Gates nodded, and his dark face split with a grin. "Be a pleasure working with you, sir."

It was not an optimum solution from a security point of view, but then, McKay reflected as he drew on his cigar, life was full of compromises, and then you died. Now that the secret of Wolf Bayou was out, *somebody* had to help guard her hidden treasure—a lot more somebodies than the Guardians and her own original security contingent together.

Like most of the survivors of the Effsee force, Gates

215

and his men had been more than happy to tear the blue-and-white FSE patches from the shoulders of their uniforms. As the sergeant put it, "We're still Americans, man."

"Yeah, Luc," Casey said. "Tom and I are going to be flying back from Washington with a load of Lee Warwick and his people in a few days. There's a salvaged plane all ready for us. Maybe you can keep that."

The former tankbuster looked glum. After piloting a genuine flying saucer, anything was going to be a letdown.

When they got back to Wolf Bayou June-Marie was so shocked to see her brother standing on the shore to greet them that she got sick to her stomach. It made Billy McKay feel pretty weird, himself. There was what you called your rational explanation, though.

Doctor Jonas "Kettle Belly" Calhoun's last note read,

> *The events of the last few hours have unveiled a side of myself I have never before permitted myself to recognize. I find I despise that which was brought squirming into the light.*
>
> *Your accusations were perfectly correct, Lieutenant McKay. I fell prey to the temptations of power—the wrong kind of power.*
>
> *I hope in my vanity that my sacrifice will still accomplish what has been and remains my goal: making Starshine available to the world. And, incidentally, makes unnecessary the futile sacrifice of your own lives.*
>
> Ave atque vale,
> *Col. Jonas N. Calhoun, U.S. Army, Ret.*

He'd simply had the Starshine security team lock Landry in a closet, and stolen *Werewolf*. The rest was history.

"Sam and I are headed down to Terrebonne," McKay said, "to see what we can do about straightening out this mess with all these damned Effsees and Cubans and shit floating around. We'll be back in a couple of days."

Landry snapped a salute. McKay snapped to attention, returned it, turned away and started off toward the landing with Jenny limping at his side.

He tripped. There was a shrill canine yell. "God *damn!*" he shouted. "Can't somebody keep this goddam Commie dog out from underfoot!"

Casey gave him a shit-eating grin. "He likes you, Billy."

Bracing herself on one crutch, Jenny bent her good leg, scooped the dog up with her free hand. "Here you go, Neruda. Say hello to your new *papa.*" She held him up to McKay.

McKay shied away. "I ain't no poppa to no Cuban mutt."

Neruda licked his face. "Looks like you're outvoted, McKay," said Sloan, cracking up.

Casting a martyred look to the heavens, McKay accepted the chubby white dog, who pumped his tail ecstatically. "This ain't the way it's supposed to work. The good guy wins, he's supposed to get the girl, not some Communist dog."

As best she could with one leg in a cast, Jeannette Robidoux sidled up to McKay and bumped his thigh with a nicely padded hip.

"You got the girl too, soldier boy."